# A SONG
# FOR KASEY

*To Shannon —*
*May Jesus give*
*you His Song in*
*your heart*
*Carole Gift Page*
*2005*

## Carole Gift Page

**MOODY PRESS**
CHICAGO

*To my beloved Grandmother Gift,*
*forever young at heart,*
*and with cherished memories*
*of Grandfather Gift,*

*To my special friend Edith Lavett,*
*ninety-one years young,*

*And in memory of my parents-in-law . . . and love,*
*Alice and Anthony Page*

---

1989 by
CAROLE GIFT PAGE

ISBN: 0-8024-8176-0

3 5 7 9 10 8 6 4 2

*Printed in the United States of America*

# 1

R . . . Y . . . A . . . N.

Dreamily, sixteen-year-old Kasey Carlone traced the name on her notebook cover. Ryan. Ryan Dimarco.

*Crazy in love with wavy brown hair smoldering brown eyes way of squinting and mouth so serious . . . that look oh that look . . . if only he were crazy in love with me too . . . .*

A noise. Voices. Commotion.

Kasey's dreamy-warm thoughts snapped. With a jarring thud, she was thrust back to cold reality—her junior class homeroom at Springfield High. She glanced up from her desk, suddenly self-conscious. The overhead lights glared harshly, bathing the classroom in a pale, impersonal haze.

Kasey shivered, although she wore her new cardigan and was not actually cold. Looking down at her notebook, she realized she had been tracing Ryan's name on the cover. With her pencil she had gone over and over each letter, so that the name stood out boldly, almost an accusation. R-Y-A-N.

Embarrassed, she covered the name with her hand. She could feel color creeping into her high cheekbones. She gazed around, but as usual no one noticed her. She had the feeling she was anonymous, invisible. If her chair were empty, it would not matter to anyone.

There was, of course, a certain benefit from being anonymous. Kasey could observe the world as if from a distance. She could watch and draw her own conclusions about things, as she was doing now. She noticed that Mr. Crane, her homeroom teacher, was absorbed in a conversation with a lank, mulish-faced boy on the Springfield High basketball team. She was aware at the same moment of voices—two boys behind her arguing about something, their voices rising and falling in anger. She glanced at the clock. Five minutes before the bell. Before her first period class.

Actually, Kasey did not mind being invisible, for she was, in her opinion, a rather plain girl. Not ugly. Ugly people were noticed almost as much as handsome people. Kasey's face was simply—unspectacular. You would miss it in a crowd. In fact, when at times she went without her glasses, she could stare directly into a mirror and see only a colorless haze. However, only during moments of unexpected vanity or weighty self-pity did she whisk off her glasses and attempt to shuffle about in a world turned joltingly impressionistic.

But if Kasey didn't have her face going for her, she figured at least she had her hands—piano hands with long, graceful fingers. She could play anything with those hands, from Beethoven and Mozart to Chopin and Debussy. But what good did that do her at Springfield High? Most of the kids here had never even heard of Chopin. They were more interested in Bruce Springsteen, Michael Jackson, and Madonna.

Without realizing it, Kasey had let her hand slip from her doodling. Ryan's name stood out boldly for all the world to see. At least, Selena Hubbard's quick eye had caught it. "Who's he—Ryan? Ryan who?" she drawled. Selena, sitting at the desk across from Kasey, was a big-boned girl at least twenty pounds overweight. She had a broad face, a pasty complexion, and a nose too large to be pretty. Leaning over intently, Selena stared at the name on Kasey's notebook. "Come on. Tell me. Who's Ryan?"

"It's nothing. Just a name," said Kasey defensively.

Selena grinned. "Sure, it's nothing. Tell me anyway."

"I was just doodling—"

"Whose name is it? Someone you like?" Selena persisted. "Let's see, who do I know named Ryan?"

Kasey covered her irritation with a forced smile. "It's nobody important. What difference does it make who he is?"

"Maybe I know him," said Selena, her black eyes snapping under her thick, unplucked brows. "Who knows? Maybe we're friends."

Kasey's heart pounded anxiously. She considered this—the possibility that Selena knew Ryan, was Ryan's friend. It didn't seem likely. But the idea was unsettling. No, Selena couldn't know Ryan. Selena was a loner. Some called her a misfit. Her wiry, coal-black hair always looked out of control, as if it had a mind of its own, and she wore oversized sweatshirts and baggy pants to disguise her girth. Kasey never saw Selena hanging out with anyone, let alone someone like Ryan Dimarco.

"I don't think you know him," Kasey said at last.

Selena wouldn't budge. "Try me. Just tell me his name, OK?"

Kasey realized that the boys behind her were no longer arguing. She stiffened. What if they were listening? Selena's voice was rising shrilly with a petulant, *"Come on, Kasey, tell me!"* Kasey had to keep her quiet.

"Well, if you must know," she whispered, "his name is—Ryan Dimarco."

Selena's face turned as animated as Silly Putty. "Hey, I do know him! See, what'd I tell you? Ryan and I work together in the cafeteria during fifth period."

"You're kidding!"

"No, in fact, we're good friends. We talk all the time," Selena said excitedly. "So tell me, are you two going around together?"

Kasey's face grew warm. "No, nothing like that. We sit next to each other in English, that's all."

"But you like him. A lot."

With mounting tension, Kasey gazed down at the scrawled name on her notebook. "I—I—uh—"

"You do, don't you!" Selena was suddenly gleeful. "I'll talk to him," she squealed. "I'll find out what he thinks of you."

Kasey looked up, startled. "No, I don't think you should do that." *She could just imagine Selena cornering Ryan by the salad bar and drawling, "Hey, I know a girl who's really stoked over you!"* What if Ryan was embarrassed? Or, worse, what if he felt sorry for her? In fact, if Selena blabbed it around school, Kasey could become a regular laughingstock.

"Listen, I won't let on that you like him," Selena insisted. "Don't worry about that."

"I—I don't know—" Kasey could feel Selena's eyes on her, penetrating. There was a peculiar strength in Selena's broad, doughy face, a shrewdness behind her eyes that Kasey could not defy.

The bell clanged, and Kasey jumped to attention. She gathered her books and stood up. Her heart was pounding furiously; her throat felt dry and tight. What if Selena could do something to help her break the ice with Ryan? Wasn't it worth the risk?

"Do whatever you think," she told Selena relentingly. Then, before she changed her mind, Kasey hurried out of the room to first period.

# 2

After school Kasey headed outside to the senior parking lot. She was glad it was Monday. Maybe she could beg a ride home with her older brother, Keith. He didn't have football practice on Mondays. Otherwise, she'd have to walk home alone—as always. It wasn't a long walk—maybe a mile, maybe less—but it was lonely. She much preferred riding home in the old Buick her parents had passed on to Keith when they bought their new Camaro. Actually, the Camaro wasn't new anymore either, but since moving to their new house in Springfield (new to *them*, anyway), it would be awhile before Dad could afford another automobile. That meant Kasey and Keith had to share the Buick. But Keith, a senior, always got first dibs on the car, which meant Kasey rarely got behind the wheel.

She spotted Keith already in the car, engine running. She raced after him, shouting, "Keith! Keith, wait!" He must have heard her or caught sight of her in the rearview mirror, because he reached over and opened the passenger door.

"You just made it, Kasey," he said above the raucous, pulsating beat blasting from his new tape deck—a song Kasey detested—Chuck Berry's "Roll over Beethoven." Keith was always listening to old rhythm and blues songs from the fifties. (He considered himself something of an expert on the fifties, rattling off statistics on names, dates, and tunes at the slightest invitation.) He had worked two months as a boxboy at Tiptop Grocery to buy the tape deck; he was a good worker, Dad always said so, but not so good at saving; he'd rather spend his money on the latest gadgets. Dad's word. Nobody else said *gadgets* anymore.

"Hey, Keith, where are the earplugs?" Kasey declared as she climbed in beside him.

"In your ears, dork." Keith's small, intense brown eyes glowered at her under thick, low-slung brows. Even with his scowl, Keith had a sturdy, chiseled face full of character and stability, a jutting chin, and straight, straw-blond hair combed over his forehead in a brush style. And he had the brawny, muscular strength of a star athlete. Maybe that was why he made the football team on his first try. "Hey, Goggles, what's with you today, huh?" (He'd teasingly called her that since she got her glasses three years ago; she hated the word!) "I said, what's up, Goggles?"

"Nothing's up. Totally nothing. A totally nothing day." Kasey adjusted the mountain of books on her lap and buckled her seatbelt, then made a flourish of turning down the music.

"Hey, I was listening to that," Keith protested.

"Yeah. So were all the cars in a one-mile radius," she snapped.

He shifted into reverse and jerked backward, then slammed the car into drive and roared out of the parking lot. Kasey's well-worn Bible and two textbooks slid off her lap. "What's *your* problem, big brother? Just get your racing wheels?"

"It's not me, Sis. It's *you.*"

"Me? What's me?"

"Your attitude. You get in the car with your face dragging, then you grump around, make wise cracks, and turn off my music just because it's not your classical, highbrow stuff."

"That's what's bugging you. I turned off your music."

"No. The fact is, it's the way you've been acting for weeks now, always moping around like you lost your last friend, like the whole world dumped on you or something—"

"It did—and I did."

"Did what?"

"Lost my last friend—and got dumped on."

Keith eased his foot on the gas pedal and looked over at her. "What you're saying is you're all bent out of shape just because we moved here to Springfield."

She stared ahead and jutted out her lower lip. "Am not."

"You are too. You hate it here. I see it in your eyes every time I look at you. And so do Mom and Dad."

She looked sharply at him. "Did they say something? What did they say?"

"Nothing. You know they wouldn't talk to me about it. Except Mom asked me once if I thought you were happy here."

"What'd you say?"

"What could I say? I couldn't lie. I just said, 'I don't know. Why don't you ask her?'"

Kasey retrieved her three toppled books. "If you ask me, Mom and Dad aren't any happier here than I am."

"Says who?"

"Come on, Keith. You've heard Dad complain about his new job. It's not like when he owned the store back home. He was his own boss then. He loved that old store as much as we did."

"As much as *you* did, you mean. I never loved that store. It was just a lot of hard work. Dad couldn't have gotten by without our help. At least here in Springfield we can live our own lives for a change."

"Yeah. Big deal. Some life. Here in Springfield I feel like a—a zoid, a big zero. X-double-minus. Plain vanilla. I might as well be invisible."

He glanced at her, then back at the road. "Invisible? Plain vanilla? Come on. What's this garbage?"

"Nothing. Forget I said it."

"No. Tell me."

She heaved a sigh. "It means that back in Middleton I felt like somebody. I had friends. I had the store. I had my music—"

"You still have your music. You've got a good piano teacher here, don't you?—maybe even better than the one in Middleton. And they've already got you playing at church."

"Sure. For the little kids—junior and primary church. In Middleton I played at all the services. I played better than anyone in town. Everyone said so."

Keith uttered a mocking little laugh. "Ah, now I see. You can't stand the competition here in Springfield. In Middleton you were a big fish in a little pond. Here, you're just a little fish—"

She jabbed him angrily. "Keith Carlone, shut your fat mouth. You don't know anything about it!"

They drove on in an uneasy silence until they reached Wildwood Drive. Their rambling, country-style two-story was on the wide corner lot. Keith pulled into the driveway, turned off the ignition, and gazed soberly at Kasey. "Listen, Kasey, maybe I was out of line to say anything. Honest, I wasn't trying to give you a hard time. It's just that I know how important playing the piano is to you. You've dreamed all your life of becoming a concert pianist, but—"

She bit her lower lip. "Are you saying that dream's too important to me?"

"No, but I know you have this thing about being the best—"

She swallowed a sudden ache in her throat. "I—I don't have to worry about being the best at anything anymore, Keith. Nobody cares. Nobody even knows I exist. Let's face it. I'm nothing but a failure. I don't even have any friends."

Keith reached out tentatively and squeezed her shoulder. "It doesn't have to be that way, Sis. Just get out there and make friends. I did."

"I'm not you, Keith. It's easy for you. You've got football. You're a star athlete. And you're good-looking and outgoing and confident. Everyone likes you."

"They'll like you too, Kasey, if you give them a chance. Look, you've never been a—a wallflower. You had lots of friends in Middleton—Sandy, Joyce, Diana—"

"Sure. We were friends all our lives. But I never had to go out and make *new* friends. The kids here—they're different. They're so—so worldly and sophisticated."

"Yeah, maybe so, but why should that bother you, Kasey?"

She hesitated, then blurted, "Because, the—the other day when I walked by a group of popular girls, I heard them call me 'hayseed' and 'country girl.'" Her voice wavered now, sounding plaintive and whiny. She hated that sound in her voice. "They laughed at me, Keith. No one ever laughed at me in Middleton."

Unexpectedly, Keith reached over and gave her an impulsive bearhug. "Listen, Kasey, if anybody gives you a hard time again, let me at 'em. I'll take 'em down a peg or two."

Kasey drew back and stared dumbstruck at her brother. Keith was usually always the big brave man, rarely one to show affection. Suddenly she wanted to cry, confide in him, spill out all her hurts. She opened the car door and stepped out, hugging her books to her chest. "Keith, before we go inside—"

He came around and scooped up her books on top of his, surprising her again. "Yeah?"

"I wasn't going to tell you, but maybe—"

"What? Tell me." There was something gentle in his voice inviting her to go on.

"There is someone here in Springfield. Someone I like."

"Oh, hey, I can tell by the look in your eyes, it's a guy, isn't it? Kasey—you, of all people! You have a guy. A special guy!"

"He—he doesn't even know I exist, Keith. Not yet anyway. But maybe he will —"

"Great!" For a moment Keith looked amused, but he grew serious again. "You got a plan, some way of making him discover you?"

"I—no, but listen—I said something dumb. Maybe I shouldn't have, but I told someone about him, someone who knows him. She's going to talk to him, Keith. I'm so nervous I feel like I'm going to jump out of my skin."

"Nervous?" He winked. "What's to be nervous about? Play it cool, Sis."

"But I'm scared."

"Scared?"

"Yeah. Scared she'll talk to him—and scared she won't."

# 3

As usual when Kasey arrived home from school, she went directly to the kitchen. She knew that's where she'd find her mother at this time of day. Sure enough, her mother stood at the kitchen counter dipping chicken pieces into batter. She looked around and smiled as Kasey approached. Her short, coppery brown hair was brushed back casually around her ears and her face glowed with a natural beauty Kasey secretly envied.

"Hi, Kasey," she said with her usual easy warmth. "How was your day?"

Kasey shrugged. "OK."

"Just OK?"

"I got an A on my term paper and an A- on my history exam."

Her mother beamed. "Well, listen here, that's something to celebrate. It just so happens I baked a marble fudge cake. Your favorite, if my memory's not too rusty."

Kasey nodded without enthusiasm. "Yeah, my favorite."

Her mother turned back to her chicken and batter. "Kasey, get me the shortening out of the pantry, OK?"

"Sure, Mom. You need some help with dinner?"

"No, we're eating late. Dad has to work overtime—again. Why don't you get in some piano practice?"

Kasey hesitated. "Maybe later, Mom. I'm not in the mood now."

"Not in the mood? Is that *my* Kasey speaking?"

"Really, Mom, I just want to crash for a while in my room." She grabbed a handful of potato chips and ran for the stairway before her mother could protest.

She slipped into her room and shut the door behind her, dropping her books on the rocking chair. Then she stretched out on her bed and cupped her hands under her head and stared at the ceiling. Automatically her mind traveled back to Middleton, the quaint little farming community she'd lived in since her birth. It was only 400 miles from Springfield, but it was a lifetime away now. Actually it had been only two months since her family packed all their belongings in a moving van and headed east to this busy, thriving city that dwarfed her slow-paced, bucolic hometown.

In Middleton life was safe and predictable. Kasey knew who—and what—she could count on. She loved working at her dad's old-fashioned general store and sharing in the lives of the customers. There she could talk freely, confidently. She knew almost everyone in town—by face, if not by name. And everyone knew and accepted her. There had been no need to compete for attention or recognition or friends. There was no fear of being rejected. It was a fact. In Middleton, everyone liked Kasey Carlone; everyone admired her, even though she was quiet and shy. Even though her piano keys did most of the talking.

She could still recall how friends and acquaintances in Middleton praised her after she played a difficult Mozart concerto in church one Sunday. *Kasey's terrific! Did you see her fingers flying over those keys? . . . Yes, that child has a distinguished career ahead of her . . . . Why, that girl's going to put Middleton on the map someday. Mark my words.*

How Kasey wished it were true. But when her mother told the choir director at their new church that Kasey was available to play, he simply said, "Oh, well, thank you, Mrs. Carlone, but we already have a full-time pianist. But I'm sure the children's church could use Kasey occasionally."

So now she played "Jesus Loves Me" for chattering, wiggly little kids who wouldn't know the difference between a Mozart concerto and the Gummi Bears' theme song.

Kasey blinked, fought tears as she stared at the ceiling. Aloud, she said, "Dear Jesus, why did You let us move here? Why couldn't we stay in Middleton? Everything was perfect there."

Well, maybe not perfect. No place was perfect. But in Kasey's memory Middleton seemed wonderfully idyllic, especially compared to life in Springfield. Here she had no friends, no way of sharing in people's lives, no chance to perform her lovely, lilting concertos. Here in Springfield everyone seemed noisier and busier and more aggressive. It wasn't enough to be simply kind and pleasant and a dutiful student. To be accepted, one had to be glamorous and popular, talented and clever, the best at everything. In Middleton, Kasey had known a measure of success; here in Springfield, she felt totally awkward, tongue-tied, plain, and inadequate. In other words, a failure!

At dinner that evening Kasey tried to keep her dismal mood to herself. No sense upsetting Mom and Dad. They had enough problems and adjustments of their own. In fact, Dad was talking as usual about the unexpected pressures of being a sales manager at F & L—the prestigious Fieffer-Leighten chain of department stores.

"We got another official proclamation from the central office," he said wearily. "They didn't like our recent ad campaign—the one I'd approved. What's worse, they're finding fault with several of our buyers, saying they're not in step, not on top of the trends—"

"But, Tony, I thought sales were up," said Mom, handing him the platter of fried chicken.

"They are, but it's a seasonal thing. Sales are always higher in the fall, before Christmas. This year sales percentages aren't as good as last year, so you know who gets the flak—"

"Yeah. The sales manager." Keith sounded perturbed. "It's not fair, Dad. You've only been there two months. What do they expect?"

"Perfection, I guess, Keith."

"So what does it all mean?" asked Mom.

"It means I try harder, work longer hours, and break my back until we get on track. It should help with Christmas just two months away. Unless the economy takes a nose dive. Then it's anybody's game."

Kasey scowled. "Back in Middleton, we didn't have to worry about ad campaigns or sales figures. We just had to make sure we had Mrs. Cather's favorite cough syrup on hand and plenty of blue yarn for Mrs. Crouse, and—"

"Yeah," said Keith, "but what prestige was there in running a dumpy little general store?"

"It wasn't dumpy!" Kasey protested.

"Hold it, you two," ordered Dad. "Let's talk about something besides my job, OK?" He looked over at Mom. "How about it, Deb? How was your day?"

"Don't ask." She laughed ironically. "I made a social call on several of our neighbors."

17

"That's great, Mom," said Kasey. "It's about time we got acquainted. I mean, they sure haven't beat a path to our doorstep to welcome us here."

"Well, now I know why," said Mom. "They all work."

"You mean you didn't find any housewives at home?" asked Dad.

"Only one, and that visit was a disaster!"

"How come?" asked Kasey.

"Well, it was Mrs. Glover, just down the street. She was laid off last week, and she's already climbing the walls. She couldn't believe I don't work outside the home."

"See, Mom?" Keith winked. "You're just not a liberated woman."

"I'm as liberated as I want to be, young man."

"So what did you say to her, Mom?" asked Kasey.

Mom's face colored. "Well, I asked if she'd be interested in joining me for a morning coffee klatch or a weekly Bible study—"

"And?"

"And—she laughed. She said she didn't know anyone in the neighborhood who would have time for such things, even in the evenings. Everyone's exhausted after a long day of work."

"Well, you work too," said Dad. "Look how hard you work to provide a comfortable home for all of us."

"I know, but Mrs. Glover made me feel like—like a second-class citizen, an anachronism."

"A what, Mom?" quizzed Keith.

"A social dinosaur. She actually accused me of setting women's lib back sixty years."

"You're kidding!" said Dad.

"Well, she said it like she was joking, but I know she meant every word."

"You used to work at the store in Middleton some-times, Mom," said Kasey. "Doesn't that count?"

"Sure, I used to pitch in when Dad needed me, but that wasn't a daily nine-to-five job."

"Debra, are you saying you want to get an outside job?" asked Dad.

Mom nudged him playfully. "Are you kidding? I like being home. I know when I've got a good deal."

"So do we. Right, kids?"

"Boy, do we!" said Keith.

Kasey nodded.

In the silence that followed, as Kasey toyed with her food, she considered telling her parents about Ryan Di-marco. She wanted to tell them how she felt about this quiet, sensitive boy who sat beside her in English. Wanted to explain that she had never felt this way about any other boy, and that maybe, just maybe, Selena Hubbard could help her get to know him. But no. She wouldn't mention Ryan or Selena yet. Wait until something happened.

Or maybe nothing would happen. Maybe Selena wouldn't talk to Ryan. Or maybe he wouldn't like Kasey, would laugh at her, would think she was dumb to care about him.

There was no way of knowing about Ryan Dimarco tonight, but tomorrow . . . tomorrow . . . anything was possible tomorrow!

# 4

Kasey arrived early in homeroom the next morning. She refused to admit how eager she was to see Selena and learn about her conversation with Ryan. Of course, it was possible that Selena had forgotten about Kasey by fifth period. She might have said nothing at all. Or perhaps Ryan did not even recall a girl named Kasey Carlone.

Still, the thought that Selena might have news about Ryan pulled at Kasey's mind, tantalizing her with dreamlike possibilities. In fact, she had thought of little but Ryan since yesterday morning.

Now, waiting for Selena to arrive, Kasey chastened herself for being so hopeful. There was no reason to hope. Since the beginning of the school year Kasey had adored Ryan from afar, and not once had he done anything to encourage her affection.

But at least the fact that someone else knew about her feelings for Ryan stirred a cautious excitement inside her. Perhaps her life here in Springfield would not always be so static, so uneventful, so dismaying.

"Guess what!" cried Selena, slipping into her seat with an air of triumph.

Kasey looked over, startled. She hadn't seen Selena enter the room. "What?" she asked, her breath suddenly trapped inside her.

Selena leaned over conspiratorially, her eyes blazing like hot coals. "I talked to him," she announced smugly. "I talked to him about *you*."

Kasey could barely utter the words. "What—did he say?"

Selena sat back, assuming a mild air of indifference. "Oh, he said a lot. We talked for a long time."

"Tell me," Kasey whispered urgently. There was a tingling in her wrists that seemed to be racing upward into her head.

"He likes you," said Selena carelessly, as if she had only commented on the weather. "That's what he said."

"Likes me?" echoed Kasey in disbelief.

Selena nodded. "He said you're a very sweet girl, and very shy, but one of the nicest girls he knows. He says you're not a silly chatterbox like some girls who go around giggling and stuff. You're serious and a good student, and he likes that."

"He said all that?" Kasey could feel her eyes widening like saucers. For an instant she felt an impulse to shout, but instead she gave way to a grin. "He really said that!" she marveled.

"Every word," said Selena.

Kasey thought a moment. "But what did you tell him about me?"

Selena shrugged. "Hardly anything. Just that you think he's really cool, that's all. That's enough to start with."

Kasey spoke over a lump in her throat. "Thanks, Selena. You don't know—I mean, I am so—I mean, this is absolutely terrific!"

The next few days were the happiest Kasey had known in Springfield. She felt as if she were walking in a dream. It was as if she could feel herself being transformed into someone else, someone important, someone Ryan Dimarco liked. In class, sitting next to him, she allowed herself to steal frequent sidelong glances, absorbing into her vision the various images of Ryan. Ryan staring thoughtfully at the chalkboard. Ryan chuckling at some joke the teacher made. Ryan smiling casually in her direction or perhaps directly at her!

Ryan had the natural, swarthy good looks of his Latin heritage, with a thick crop of dark, wavy hair and smoldering brown-black eyes nearly hidden by heavy brows. He had a way of squinting at the world with a dubious, self-protective scrutiny, as if he wasn't about to let anyone read him too quickly or too easily. But that didn't matter to Kasey. She knew the truth. It was their secret. Ryan cared for her, maybe even considered her his girl!

It was impossible to concentrate on schoolwork now. Kasey's assignments loomed in her mind like a mountain she must scale, a terrible, unthinkable effort. She would much rather remain in the pastel valley of her dreams. When she rose each morning, she uttered a special prayer for Ryan. When she practiced the piano each evening she imagined that she was playing for Ryan alone. When she sat at the dinner table with her parents and brother, her mind constantly strayed to thoughts of Ryan, until one evening her mother felt her forehead and asked if she was coming down with the flu.

"Of course not," Kasey replied. "I've never felt better in my life!"

And it was true. All because of Ryan.

Kasey weighed every word Ryan spoke to her, every glance, every smile. What did they mean? What did they promise? What sort of world lay ahead for Kasey that she had never dared wish for before?

Of course, nothing had actually happened—outwardly. Ryan said or did nothing to indicate that he had special feelings for her. He was as pleasant as he had always been, but not especially attentive.

When Kasey mentioned this fact to Selena at lunch one day, Selena replied without a second thought. "Of course he's not going to let you see how he feels until he knows how you feel about him. He's no nerd, you know."

"But I'm crazy about him—he must know that," Kasey fretted. "Doesn't he know how I feel?"

"I'll tell him," said Selena, unwrapping a peanut butter sandwich from her lunch sack. She took a large bite and chewed noisily. "Don't worry, Kasey. I'll let him know."

After that, Kasey and Selena met often to compare notes on Ryan Dimarco. There were moments during homeroom period, of course, but they seemed hardly long enough. Each day Selena had new information—where Ryan lived, what church he attended (Springfield Bible), what hobbies he enjoyed. "He's the oldest of five children," she told Kasey, "so he's really mature for his age. He helps out at home and works part-time, and he studies like crazy so he can get a scholarship and go to a good college. Face it, Kasey, he's one cool dude."

So eager was Kasey to discuss Ryan that she and Selena began to meet regularly during lunch hour, and eventually they began to walk home from school together. They had developed an unusual friendship based on Selena's obvious pleasure in delivering bits of information about Ryan and Kasey's enormous gratitude in receiving these treasured reports.

The strange thing was that, for the most part, Kasey's relationship—or nonrelationship—with Ryan remained unchanged. They chatted briefly before or after class and, during class, exchanged quick, sly smiles, which Kasey cherished in her memory long after class was dismissed. But their conversation was mostly superficial, about test scores and assignments and routine school gossip. Whenever Kasey asked Ryan a question about himself or his interests, he always answered with a pleasant grin, but he rarely asked her anything about herself.

One noon, while Selena tore the cellophane wrapping off a chocolate cupcake and methodically stuffed the delicacy into her mouth, Kasey, sitting across from her, asked, "If Ryan really likes me, why doesn't he ever ask me out?"

Selena licked the crumbs from her lips and answered, "I thought I explained that."

Kasey shook her head. "No, you never did."

Selena sat hunched forward with both elbows on the table. "I'll tell you," she said, glancing around as if to be sure no one was listening. "His mother doesn't want him to date anyone. He's a brain, you know, and she's afraid a girl might distract him from his studies. He feels bad about not being able to ask you out, but there's nothing he can do. His mom's a regular shrew."

"I see," Kasey murmured, but she wasn't sure that she did.

# 5

Selena finished her lunch early as usual, because she worked in the cafeteria fifth period and had to be in the kitchen dressed in her uniform at exactly 12:45 P.M. "I'll be standing right alongside Ryan," she reminded Kasey, with a gleeful little smile.

"Tell him I said hi," said Kasey as Selena lumbered off with her lunch tray.

As Kasey swallowed the last of her tapioca pudding, she heard a rustling sound. She looked over in surprise as a classmate sat down beside her—a girl she had seen often but never spoken to. The girl wore hearing aids in both ears and used sign language with one or two other deaf students, but Kasey had never heard her speak. Since Kasey's classmates never talked to the girl, Kasey assumed she couldn't speak, so she did a double take when the girl said, "Hi, Kasey."

"Hi," Kasey said back in a loud, startled voice.

The girl smiled. She was a tall, angular girl with a lean face and distinctive, sharply carved features—a long nose, high cheekbones, a generous chin, small, snapping eyes, and fine chestnut-brown hair. "My name is—Jenny Clegg," she said slowly, her words falling with a thick, blunt-edged distortion.

"I didn't know you talked," Kasey blurted, then covered her mouth in embarrassment.

"Yes, I talk," said Jenny with an amused smile. "But, please, don't cover your mouth. I read lips."

"I—I'm sorry. I'm Kasey Carlone. I've seen you around—"

"We are in history together," said Jenny. "You are smart. You always know the answers."

"Not always," said Kasey. "But I do like history."

"Me too. But it's hard."

Kasey glanced at Jenny's hearing aids. "Yeah, I guess it would be. How do you do it?"

Jenny tapped her temple beside her eyes. "I watch the teacher every minute. I read his lips and memorize what he says. And I read lots of books. I learn more than I must know for the tests."

"But why don't you ever speak in class? I bet the teacher doesn't know you can."

Jenny's dark brown eyes grew serious. "People don't like the way I sound. I sound funny. So they think I'm dumb."

"But anyone can see you're not dumb," said Kasey. "All they have to do is listen to what you say."

"Not many people have time to listen."

Kasey glanced up at the wall clock. "Wow, speaking of time—"

"I know. It's time for fifth period. But I wanted to say—"

Kasey gathered up her books and looked expectantly at Jenny. "Yes?"

"I want to tell you—this is not easy—"

"What, Jenny? What's wrong?"

"I see you every day with your friend—"

"My friend? You mean Selena?"

"Yes. Sometimes—I shouldn't—but I read her lips. I see what she tells you."

Kasey shifted her books impatiently. "I don't understand, Jenny. Is there some problem with Selena?"

Jenny pushed back the fine spray of bangs across her forehead. Her eyes darted around the room as if she were seeking some invisible answer in the walls. "I better not— maybe it is OK—"

"What, Jenny? What are you talking about?"

Jenny made a clicking sound with her mouth and shook her head, flustered. "You be careful, Kasey. Watch out. Don't get hurt."

"I won't. But what's that got to do with Selena? What aren't you telling me, Jenny?"

With a helpless shrug, Jenny pivoted, bumped against a table, then rushed away without a backward glance. Kasey called after her, then caught herself, realizing in embarrassment that Jenny couldn't hear her.

Kasey puzzled over Jenny's veiled warning all afternoon—until English class. Then, as usual, all she could think about was Ryan. Ryan sitting just across from her. Ryan smiling his usual wonderful smile.

But today was even better than she had anticipated. Better than her wildest dreams. When the dismissal bell rang, Ryan walked her out of class and stood with her in the hallway, talking confidentially.

"Listen, Kasey," he said in his smooth, easy-going voice, "I've been planning something special for Friday evening. It's been in the works for a couple of weeks now, and I was just thinking that it's something you might really enjoy. Are you busy on Friday?"

"Busy? Uh, no." Her heart was hammering so loud she couldn't hear her own voice. "No, I'm not doing a thing Friday night."

"Great. Then why don't I pick you up about seven, OK?" He turned to go.

"But—but you don't know where I live."

"Oh, just give me your address in class tomorrow."

"Yeah, sure," she said breathlessly. "I'll do that."

Kasey could scarcely wait for the school day to end so that she could meet Selena and share this latest, most fantastic development concerning Ryan. She felt like Dorothy in *The Wizard of Oz* stepping from her drab black-and-white Kansas cottage into the glorious, Technicolor Emerald City. Imagine, just imagine! An actual date with Ryan Dimarco—yes, a whole evening alone with the boy she adored!

Selena was incredulous. Her coal-black eyes bulged slightly as her unplucked brows shot up in astonishment. "You're kidding, Kasey. You mean Ryan actually asked you out?"

"Yes, isn't it absolutely the most wonderful thing?"

"You're sure he meant a real date?"

"Yes, of course. He said he's been planning it for weeks!"

Selena looked dubious. "Where is he taking you?"

Kasey shrugged, breathless with exhilaration. "I don't know. He didn't say. He just said he knew it was something I would enjoy."

Selena trudged along, her head down, kicking at stones. Her baggy sweatshirt and faded jeans seemed sloppier than ever. "I can't believe it—"

"Why not, Selena?" Kasey's voice was buoyant, her spirits soaring. "After all, you're the one who made it happen. I have you to thank, Selena! You were right about Ryan, right about us belonging together. I never would have had the courage to hope if it weren't for you."

"I—I don't know what to say," Selena stammered.

"You don't have to say anything," said Kasey, feeling generous and deliriously euphoric. She sucked in her breath and declared, "Right this minute, Selena, thanks to you, I'm the happiest girl on earth!"

# 6

On Friday evening, Kasey felt as if a power beyond her control pulsed through her veins—an extreme nervousness, a frenzy of anticipation. The night hovered before her like a lovely mystery. Surely she was not actually preparing for a date with Ryan Dimarco—dabbing perfume on her wrists and brushing her wheat-brown, shoulder-length hair for him. Impossible, but true.

She studied her reflection in the dresser mirror. Without her glasses, her lean, angular face looked like a hazy, pastel egg. She could barely make out her pale, gray-blue eyes or her feathery brows bleached by the sun. Her unruly mane of hair, with its sun-faded streaks, was the color of cornbread and molasses. She sighed in exasperation. Forget brushing. Her hair seemed to have a mind of its own, with stubborn cowlicks sending it off in several directions at once. Maybe Ryan would consider it the windswept look.

But what about her glasses? Should she wear them? If she did, she wouldn't look special, just studious. But if she left them off, she might miss Ryan, or miss a step, or worse. Better wear them.

Kasey slipped eagerly into her one and only cashmere sweater and wrap-around skirt. With her nylons and stacked heels she looked older. Maybe even eighteen. Her life was changing. Tonight proved it. There was more to living than what she had known. More. Perhaps endless possibilities. And now they stood practically within her grasp. God was blessing her. He was showing her that it was not necessary, after all, to be anonymous, to live an invisible life—not even here in Springfield.

Then, before Kasey was even ready, the evening began. The doorbell rang, and, moving as if in a dream, Kasey went to answer it. She opened the door, but it was not Ryan who greeted her. She stared in confusion at Nancy Hart, a girl from school whose bouncy personality always vibrated an appealing energy.

"You ready, Kasey?" Nancy chirped while Kasey stood open-mouthed.

"Ready?" Kasey echoed without comprehension.

With a wave of her hand, Nancy gestured toward the waiting automobile. "You better hurry. Ryan has the engine running. You know him—always in a rush. Wait'll you see that car, Kasey. It's crammed. Ryan must have invited everyone in the school."

"For our date?" Kasey blurted.

Nancy gave her a quizzical glance. "Ryan did tell you where we're going, didn't he?"

Kasey struggled to recover from her blunder. No one must know that she was expecting a date with Ryan tonight. "Uh, no, Ryan didn't exactly say where we were going."

Nancy laughed. "That's Ryan for you. He expects everyone to read his mind. We're going to Shady Oaks."

Kasey was as puzzled as ever. "Shady Oaks?"

Nancy rolled her eyes. "Boy, he really did leave you in the dark, didn't he?" Nancy started back down the steps. "It's an old folks' home, Kasey. Come on. We're supposed to be there by seven."

Kasey grabbed her purse, called good-bye to her mother, and hurried down the steps after Nancy. Sure enough, Ryan's car was bursting with youthful, exuberant humanity. In other words, gorgeous girls.

Kasey swallowed her disappointment and managed a cheery hello as she squeezed into the back seat between two of the popular girls from school.

Ryan looked around and grinned. "Hi, Kasey. I'm glad you could make it. I think you know everyone, don't you?"

Kasey looked around. She could feel her face flushing with embarrassment. "Well, yes, I—I guess I do."

"Great." Ryan turned back to the wheel and put the car in reverse. "Listen, gang," he continued as he pulled out onto the street, "here's our plan. We'll read a few verses—Psalms is good, OK?—sing a few songs, and who-ever wants to, or is willing, can say something. We'll keep it casual and friendly, nothing too formal, got it?"

Kasey looked at the girl beside her—Janice some-thing; she was in Kasey and Ryan's English class too. "We're putting on a program?" Kasey asked tentatively. "For the old people?"

Janice nodded. "You didn't know? Yeah, we do this about once a month. Sometimes our whole youth group from Community Bible goes; sometimes just a few of us."

"Oh, I see," said Kasey. "I didn't realize—"

Janice leaned against the front seat and nudged Ryan. "How come you didn't tell Kasey where we were going?"

Ryan glanced up into the rearview mirror and met Kasey's gaze. "Hey, Kasey, listen, I'm sorry," he said earnestly. "I figured everyone knew about our treks to the retirement home. And when I saw you carrying your Bible at school, I had a feeling you'd fit right into our group. I hope I wasn't assuming too much."

"Oh, no, not at all. I mean, I'm glad you asked me."

"Great. I'm glad too. Our visits mean a lot to these old-timers." Ryan's voice took on a tender edge as he added, "My grandfather lived at Shady Oaks for a while—until he died last year. That's how I got to know the folks there."

Minutes later Ryan pulled up beside an ancient, Victorian-style house with arched windows and a sprawling porch across the front. Two towering oak trees stood like sentinels on each side of the sagging house, their gnarled branches fanning out like protective arms over the shingled roof.

"You can see where it gets the name 'Shady Oaks,'" said Ryan.

A face peered around the lace curtains at a window; then the door opened and a matronly woman in a crisp white uniform stepped outside and waved.

"That's Clarisa Huckabey," said Nancy. "She runs this place almost single-handed."

"And on a shoestring, according to my mom," said Ryan. "That's why they're so grateful for any help we can give them."

"Once we came out and washed windows," said Nancy, "and last Easter we brought them baskets of fresh fruits and vegetables."

"What a wonderful thing to do," said Kasey. Silently she mused that maybe these girls weren't so stuck on themselves after all. And Ryan—in spite of her disappointment over their so-called date, Kasey had to admit that he was wonderfully kind and compassionate.

As everyone piled out of the car and headed inside, Kasey fell into step beside Ryan. "I—I haven't been here before," she whispered. "I'm not sure what I'm supposed to do."

He squeezed her shoulder reassuringly. "You'll be fine. Just follow my lead."

They entered the homey living room where a dozen elderly people sat on overstuffed sofas, or in rocking chairs or wheelchairs. Some looked up expectantly and smiled; others stared into space or out the window. One woman was knitting something—a sweater perhaps; another sat clutching a rag doll and mumbling to herself.

Ryan took Kasey's hand and walked her around the room, introducing her to each person. "Mrs. Smolin, this is my friend Kasey—Mr. Suttles, Mr. Hildreth, this is Kasey—and Kasey, this is Mrs. Pinkelman and Miss Brummett." On they went, around the room, until Kasey had met each one—the white-haired little man who looked like Albert Einstein, the squat lady with a big smile and no teeth, the short, stooped woman with smiling eyes, the pillow-shaped lady with the lace shawl and flowered hat, the bald, spectacled man whose wrist shook even as he gripped Kasey's hand.

Kasey felt a lump in her throat as she thought about her own grandparents back in Middleton. She hadn't seen Grandma and Grandpa Carlone for almost three months now. How she missed them! How could she stand to let them grow old—maybe even die!—without her?

Ryan leaned over and whispered something to Kasey, drawing her back from her wistful memories.

She looked up, startled. "What?"

"I said, that lady over there in the hallway is Olive Solomon. She's not exactly sociable. She always leaves the room when we come to visit."

"Why?"

"I don't know. They say she was once a famous opera singer with thousands of fans, but now she evidently hates music—and people."

Kasey glanced over at the short, stocky woman with the deeply lined face and the fuzzy, silver-gray hair pulled back into an uneven bun. Olive Solomon had a bulbous nose, unattended brows and deep pockets of flesh under her sad, dark eyes. She reminded Kasey of newspaper photos she had once seen of the Israeli leader Prime Minister Golda Meir, except that Olive Solomon's eyes were rimmed with unspeakable despair.

Somehow Kasey felt drawn to the woman; perhaps she sensed a depth of loneliness in the solitary figure that struck a familiar chord in her own heart. Impulsively Kasey walked into the hallway and held out her hand. "Hello, Mrs. Solomon. I'm Kasey Carlone."

Olive Solomon gathered her gray sweater around her sagging frame and eyed Kasey skeptically. "Are you here to sing?"

Kasey shrugged. "I—well, yes, I guess we will be singing."

The stooped woman turned away and shuffled back down the hall with her cane. Kasey heard her mutter, "Young striplings and their daft music! Makes a body wish she *was* hard of hearing!"

Ryan touched Kasey's arm and drew her back into the living room. "Didn't I tell you?" he murmured. "She's a hard nut to crack."

Clarisa Huckabey approached with a welcoming smile and said, "Our people are ready whenever you are, Ryan. They certainly enjoy your visits."

Ryan gathered Nancy, Kasey, and Janice over to one side. "Any of you play the piano? Or do we sing Acapulco as usual?"

"A cappella, silly," said Nancy.

"Whatever." Ryan grinned.

"Count me out," said Janice. "All I can play is the radio."

"I—I play the piano, Ryan," said Kasey.

"Terrific! It's just an old upright and not exactly in tune, but if you can pound the right keys, we'll be in business."

"Sure. What do you want me to play?"

"You got me. I'm not even sure they have any sheet music here."

Kasey shrugged. "I could play one of my memorized pieces."

Ryan grinned. "Great. Go ahead. We'll start with you."

"Right now? Just like that?"

"Sure. Who knows? Maybe you can make us a class act yet."

Kasey walked over to the piano, sat down, and tried the keys. Out of tune, but it could be worse. Her face felt warm; she looked over self-consciously at Ryan. He smiled and gave her a thumbs-up sign. She relaxed a little and began to play "Chariots of Fire." As her fingers moved swiftly, liltingly over the keys, she could sense a subtle change in the room—a stirring, a brightening. All eyes were turning her way, even those that had seemed glazed and distracted.

As she played the final triumphant refrain, a burst of applause rose from the elderly residents. One grizzled gentleman rasped, "Bravo! Bravo!"

Kasey gazed around the room, basking in the unexpected acclaim. Finally, her eyes settled on a shadowed form in the hallway. Was it possible? The caustic, sharptongued Olive Solomon stood with her gnarled hands resting on her cane. Her weathered, wrinkled face shone with something besides despair—almost a wistfulness, a yearning that both baffled and intrigued Kasey. The ancient, aristocratic lady didn't utter a sound, but her eyes were glistening with what looked amazingly like admiration.

# 7

On Monday morning, Kasey entered her homeroom with mixed feelings. She dreaded telling Selena about her baffling, so-called Friday night "date" with Ryan. And yet she hoped against hope that Selena might offer some explanation for Ryan's puzzling behavior. As Kasey took her seat and swiveled toward Selena, she could tell from the expectant look on Selena's face that she was dying to hear every detail.

"Was it fabulous?" she prompted. "Was he incredibly romantic? Did he try to kiss you? Did you let him?"

"No—no—no—and no," said Kasey reluctantly.

"No? What do you mean, no?"

Kasey felt exasperated now. "I mean, no, it wasn't fabulous, he wasn't romantic, he didn't kiss me, and I didn't let him," she said dryly. "Of course, how could I let him when he didn't even ask me?"

"You're talking in riddles, Kasey. Just what did happen?"

Kasey shook her head somberly. "Well, it started out being disaster city—"

"No way! How could a date with Ryan Dimarco be a disaster?"

"Listen, Selena, it was the strangest thing," Kasey confided. "Would you believe? We went to a home for the elderly."

Selena looked absolutely bug-eyed. "A home for the who?"

"You heard me. The elderly. You know. A retirement home."

"But why? I don't get it."

"Well, it wasn't as bad as it sounds," Kasey whispered. "In fact, I actually enjoyed it. We put on this little program, and I played the piano, and the people were totally thrilled. It made me feel good inside to see how happy I made them."

"But what about Ryan? What about your date?"

"That's just it, Selena. It wasn't a date at all. At least, not what I figured a date would be. Not that I'm an expert, of course. My datebook's never been exactly crammed." She didn't add that she had never had a real date. Never a serious crush. Never even held hands. She'd always had her music and in her shyness had conveniently hidden behind it.

Selena's broad face was oddly pinched with perplexity. "But Ryan must have said something—"

"No, nothing. Except that he thought I was a terrific pianist." Kasey shrugged. "I kept expecting him to say something personal, something to let me know I was special from the other girls."

"Other girls? What other girls?"

Kasey sighed in dismay. She had let it slip. "It's just that—well, Ryan took four other girls beside me."

Selena's mouth gaped. "No way! You gotta be kidding!"

"No, I'm not. In fact, he picked me up last and took me home first. It was like he considered me nothing more than just another girl from school."

Selena settled back in her seat and lowered her head until her pudgy chin folded into her second chin. She scowled as if deliberating a very serious matter and finally looked up and nodded as if she had reached an earth-shaking conclusion.

"What is it?" asked Kasey.

"I'll get the answer for you," said Selena. "I'll talk to Ryan and find out just what little game he's playing."

Kasey shook her head slowly. "Oh, I don't think he's playing any game, Selena. Ryan is the most sincere boy I've ever met."

Selena gave Kasey an indulgent little smile and said, "You just don't know boys like I do. You meet me after school tonight, and I'll give you the facts about Ryan."

Kasey felt a little uncomfortable with the idea that Ryan might be playing a game with her—and even more uncomfortable at the prospect of trying to beat him at his own game. But what else could she do? She had to know how Ryan felt about her.

As the first bell rang, Selena cast a scrutinizing glance at Kasey. "You do still like Ryan, don't you?"

Kasey scooped up her books and nodded. "Oh, yes! More than ever. You should have seen him Friday night. He's a born leader. And he was so kind and friendly to all the old people! Oh, yes, Selena!" She cupped her hand around her mouth and whispered, "Promise you won't tell anyone, but I—I think I love him!"

At lunch that afternoon, Kasey was still painting rosy dreams of Ryan in her imagination when Jenny Clegg sat down at the table beside her. They began to talk, and before Kasey realized it, she was pouring out all her questions and confusion about Ryan and Friday night. "What do you think about Ryan, Jenny? Do you think he likes me? Or is he just playing some sort of crazy game?"

Jenny moved her hands gracefully, speaking in sign language as she sounded out the words: "Ryan is a very nice boy. He would not play games."

Kasey smiled. "That's how I feel too. And he did say he liked the way I play the piano. That's something."

Jenny brightened, her face suddenly animated. "You must let the whole school hear you play piano."

"Oh, no, I couldn't. I mean, how would I—?"

Jenny's fingers moved quickly, deftly. "You can enter the all-school piano contest next month. Maybe you will win."

"Oh, Jenny, really, I—" Kasey hesitated. Wait. Why not? Ever since she had come to Springfield she had wanted to show people what she could do, how well she could play the piano. Maybe this was her chance. Why not? The elderly people had loved her music. What better way to carve her own niche in the social system at Springfield High?

"I'll think about it, Jenny," she said with a smile. "I really will think seriously about entering the contest."

"I will be cheering for you," said Jenny.

Kasey reached out and touched Jenny's moving fingers. "I wish I could speak your language—and I wish you could hear me play the piano."

Jenny smiled knowingly. "All things are possible, Kasey. You can speak my language, and I can hear you play the piano."

Kasey wrinkled her forehead doubtfully. "How can you say that, Jenny? I know the Bible says all things are possible, but still—"

"Look," said Jenny, taking Kasey's hand and bending her fingers to reflect her own, "I will teach you signing. At lunch. Like this. Every day."

"Really? I'd love it," said Kasey. "But wait. What about the piano? You said you could hear me play. But how?"

"After lunch I will show you," said Jenny.

"Show me? How?"

"The music room is empty at lunchtime. We will go there, and you will play for me."

"If you say so." Kasey shrugged and bit into her sandwich.

"Don't look so doubtful," said Jenny. "I like music. In my church I am in the choir. We perform often for the congregation."

"You're kidding!" said Kasey. "You can sing?"

"I sing in my own way, with my hands," said Jenny with a smile. "You see, I am in a choir for the deaf. We sign while someone else sings. People say it is very beautiful to see."

"Oh, Jenny, I'd love to come see your choir perform!"

"But first, I must hear you play your piano. Today, OK?"

When they had finished eating, Kasey and Jenny gathered their books and went straight to the empty music room. The old Steinway grand piano sat in the corner beckoning Kasey to play. How she wished she could have a piano like this in her own home rather than their timid little upright.

Kasey sat down and ran her fingers lightly over the keys, then looked up at Jenny. "What do you want me to play?"

"Whatever you like." Jenny placed her hands palms-down flat on the back of the piano and closed her eyes. "I am ready to listen."

Kasey gazed questioningly at Jenny, then shrugged and began to play "El-Shaddai." Minutes later, when she had finished, she looked over at Jenny and was surprised to see a blissful smile on her face.

Eagerly Jenny sat on the piano bench beside Kasey and took her hands. "It was beautiful. You must play for the whole school."

"But how could you hear me? How could you hear the music?"

Jenny crooked her head slightly, her smile still in place. "Music is not only to be heard. It is also to be felt."

"Felt? You mean, through your hands?"

"Yes. I could feel the vibrations of your music. It was like a rolling river, with wonderful, smooth waves surging again and again over the shore. Please, Kasey, play something else."

This time Kasey played a song she had played often for her church back in Middleton, "Sing Your Praise to the Lord."

Afterward, Jenny said, "That one is like raindrops on a window, like the sun peeking through the clouds, like the wind making leaves dance."

Kasey eyed her quizzically. "You got all that from a few piano vibrations?"

Jenny laughed. "We can find beauty in many ways, Kasey, if we are open to it. Just as music is more than sound, so beauty is more than what we see."

Kasey grinned. "You, my friend, are a philosopher at heart!"

Jenny lifted Kasey's right hand and moved her fingers up, positioning them just so. She folded them down, then up again. "That spells 'beauty' in my language."

Kasey tried again, by herself. "Like this?"

"You are close. We will practice every day."

Later, as Kasey walked to her fifth period class, she reflected how odd it was that she should gain a new appreciation of music from a girl who could not hear.

As the bell rang ending fifth period, Kasey's heart began to pound nervously. She would go to English now and see Ryan. She hadn't seen him since he dropped her off at her house on Friday night, but Selena had promised to talk to him during fifth period. Had she? What had they said? Kasey wouldn't know until she talked with Selena after school.

Kasey figured that all she could do now was greet Ryan with a smile and pretend that nothing had happened, that her hopes hadn't been raised and dashed Friday night, that Selena hadn't just talked to him in fifth period and told him how much Kasey adored him (or maybe Selena had withheld that important bit of information, saving it for a better time).

Not knowing just what Ryan had been told was unsettling. Kasey glanced at him from the corner of her eye as she sat down at her desk. Maybe she could read something in his expression. Maybe this time he would say something that would give her a clue as to his true feelings for her.

But all he did was smile pleasantly and say, "Hi, Kasey. How's it going?"

"Hi, Ryan," she said softly, looking away, fighting a sudden wave of embarrassment.

"You were great Friday night," he said with unabashed enthusiasm. "The hit of the evening."

She gazed at him, her hopes rising. "You really think so?"

"Sure! The folks loved you! They don't get to hear playing like that very often."

"Oh, you mean the piano," she said with sudden disppointment.

"Yeah, sure, the piano. What else?" Before she could respond, he added, "Maybe you could join us again sometime. How about it?"

"I—I'd love to."

"Terrific. We'll probably go again in a couple of weeks. I'll give you a call."

Kasey nodded.

The bell rang to begin sixth period just as Miss O'Connor stepped to the front of the room with her attendance book in hand. Kasey pivoted in her seat and folded her hands attentively on her desk. Her face felt warm, her skin prickly. Ryan had said, "I'll give you a call." That could mean anything. The possibilities were endless. Obviously Selena had said all the right things to him during their fifth period conversation.

After school, Kasey nearly flew to the front entrance to meet Selena. She stood alone by the center door, leaning against the main pillar. They greeted each other, but Kasey forced herself to remain silent about Ryan until they were away from the milling crowd.

Finally, when she could stand it no longer, she blurted, "I've got to know! Did you find out what's going on with Ryan?"

Selena assumed her usual smug expression and said cryptically, "Maybe I did and maybe I didn't."

"Please, Selena," Kasey urged as they walked through the parking lot, "don't play games. Just tell me. Why did Ryan ask me out Friday night and then take all those other girls along? Does he like me or doesn't he? Does he know how I feel about him?"

"Hold on. One question at a time. He knows you like him a lot, and that's how he feels about you too."

Kasey felt awestruck. "How do you know? Did he say so?"

Selena nodded. "He said he had a great time with you Friday night, and he considered you his date even though he had to take the other girls too."

"But I don't understand. If he likes me, why is he keeping everything so low-key? Why doesn't he tell me himself?"

"He can't, Kasey." Selena panted. They were walking briskly, and she was obviously out of breath. She shifted her books in her arms and slackened her pace.

Kasey slowed down too, falling back into step beside Selena. "What do you mean—he can't?"

"It's like I told you before. His parents are strict. They don't want him to have a steady girl. So if he wants to see you, he has to make it look like it's not a date—like he did Friday night."

Kasey snorted. "Well, if that was supposed to be a date, he did a fantastic job of disguising the fact."

"Exactly. But what does it matter as long as the two of you know the truth?"

Kasey puzzled over Selena's argument. A date that wasn't a date but really was a date? It didn't make sense. "I don't know," she murmured. "What's the point of dating someone if no one can know?"

"It won't be forever, Kasey. Just until his parents get used to him having a girl friend. He's worth waiting for, isn't he?"

Kasey grinned. "Yeah, he is. Besides, he told me today that he'll call me sometime. He wants me to go again to Shady Oaks."

"See? What did I tell you? You just play it his way, and it'll be a perfect romance!"

# 8

At dinner that evening, Kasey told her parents that she was going to try out for the all-school piano contest. "It's open to everyone at Springfield High, but only ten students will be selected for the final play-off in December."

"I'm sure you'll have no trouble being accepted," said her father as he helped himself to the pork chops.

"We'll all come hear you," said Mom. "I'm so glad to see you regaining your interest in the piano."

"Mom, I never stopped loving the piano," said Kasey. "You know it's all I've ever dreamed of doing. It's just that since we moved to Springfield, I haven't had much chance to play in public."

"I hear you'll be up against Laury Lassen," said Keith in his teasing, big brother voice. "Looks like you've got your work cut out for you, Goggles."

Kasey bristled. "Mom, he's saying that again. Make him stop!"

"That's enough, Keith," said Dad. "You know how your sister feels about that—that word—"

"It's just a little term of endearment, Sis. No big deal, OK?"

"How would you like it if I called you 'Moose-face?'"

"Come on, you two. Cool it," said Mom. "Now what's this about Laury Lassen? Who's she?"

Keith reached for the fried potatoes. "Laury Lassen is just the hottest girl in school, that's all. She's got these fantastic eyes and long black hair. And I hear she plays a real mean piano."

"Well, sure, I hear Laury's pretty good," said Kasey, annoyed, "but—"

"Good? You kidding? They say no one can come close to her. She's awesome!"

"Awesome? You mean she's gorgeous," said Kasey cynically. "That doesn't mean she's the best pianist."

"True," said Keith, between bites. "The piano contest will prove that."

Kasey swatted him with her napkin. "Keith Carlone, whose side are you on anyway?"

"Your side!" he exclaimed, ducking. "I want you to win, Sis, but I think you should know what you're up against."

"Don't do me any favors, big brother." Kasey picked up her fork and jabbed at her pork chop. She wasn't about to tell Keith that Laury Lassen was one of the girls who had called her 'hayseed' and 'country girl.' In fact, she led the popular clique at school that shunned girls like Kasey and Selena Hubbard and Jenny Clegg.

Laury Lassen always spoke with the deliberate, dramatic flair of an actress and moved with the practiced poise of a model. But, frankly, Kasey found her aloofness and smugness both irritating and intimidating. Still, all the

48

boys adored Laury, and the girls envied her and vied for her approval, so what chance did Kasey have against her?

Except talent. Kasey had to believe she was more talented than Laury. Surely, Laury had some fatal flaw somewhere; she couldn't be perfect, could she?

"I'll win the piano competition," Kasey said aloud, glaring defiantly at Keith. "I'll win. You just wait and see."

Keith raised his hands in mock surrender. "Sure you will, Kase. You're Middleton's best."

Mom nodded. "I really believe you will win, Kasey. But that means you'd better get busy practicing."

"Oh, I will, Mom. I will. Starting tonight."

"I hear Laury Lassen doesn't even have to practice," said Keith in the glib, needling tone he assumed when he was determined to outmaneuver his sister. "They say she just plays naturally with hardly any effort at all."

"I find that hard to believe," said Dad, spearing another chop.

"No one wins competitions without practice," said Mom, "no matter how good they are."

"No, really. I heard her say so," said Keith. "I heard her tell some girls that she never practices except for a few minutes before her lesson each week. Laury just has a natural gift."

Kasey pretended to choke. "Laury has—what?"

"Read my lips, Bozo-brains. I said she has a natural gift."

"Sounds more like she has a puppy dog panting at her heels," said Kasey. "Meaning you, big brother. You've got it bad."

"Hit the road, toad. I'm not scamming on Laury Lassen, if that's what you think!"

"Sure you are! You and every other guy at Springfield High. But I bet underneath that femme fatale image, she's a regular Betty Boop." To underscore her point, Kasey made a Kewpie doll face at Keith and squealed, "Boop-oop-a-doop!"

The tendon along Keith's jawline tightened. "Listen, Sis, I don't need to hit on Laury Lassen or any of her fast-lane chicks. I've got plenty of cute girls that like me just fine."

"Yeah, I know," Kasey shot back mockingly. "I see you at school, super jock. You're always surrounded by gawking, preening groupie-types who idolize anything in a football jersey."

Keith's face reddened, and his temples pulsed. "Is that so? Well, I see you around school too, Sis, and the only groupies you've got are either fat or deaf!"

"Keith! That's enough!" Kasey's father bellowed.

The dining room rang with a sudden, electrifying silence. Mom and Dad both glared disapprovingly at Keith. Kasey felt a sob rise in her throat. She pushed back her chair and tried to stand, but her eyes blurred with tears. Her chair toppled with a bang as she stumbled blindly from the table. Before she could escape, Keith reached out and seized her arm.

His voice was resonant with regret. "Wait, Kase. I'm sorry."

She stood waiting numbly while Keith set her chair upright and guided her back into it. He put a broad hand on her shoulder and squeezed apologetically.

"Listen, I didn't mean what I said. I don't even know what made me say it. It's just that I noticed the Hubbard girl and Jenny Clegg seem to be the only friends you have."

Kasey brushed away tears of humiliation. "Yes, they are my friends. They're wonderful friends. So what's wrong with that? Just because they're not popular—just because they're different? So I'm different too, Keith. I'm

50

plain and awkward and shy and tongue-tied when I want to be sophisticated and witty, but I hope nobody ever says to you, Keith, 'You mean that plain, skinny girl is the only sister you've got?'"

"Your sister's absolutely right, son," said Dad. "I hope you're not letting yourself get brainwashed by this 'popularity is everything' attitude so many people have today."

"Dad, I'm not. Believe me," said Keith. "It just irked me that Kasey would think I'd fall for someone like Laury Lassen. I see through her. I know she's got as much depth as a postage stamp—"

"Listen, Keith—Kasey," said Mom. "I don't think either of you intended to turn what began as good-humored teasing into something combative. Let's forget the Lassen girl and school and piano contests right now and talk about something else."

"Sure, Mom," said Kasey, her voice still edged with melancholy. "What do you want to talk about?"

"Well, for one thing, I've found a way for you to earn a little extra money."

"Extra money? You mean a part-time job? What is it?"

"It won't take much time, just an hour or so a week."

"What, Mom? Tell me!"

"I've found a couple of neighborhood children who want to take piano lessons."

Kasey stared at her mother. "You've roped me into teaching piano to a couple of kids? Mom, I bet they're insufferable brats."

"No, they're very sweet children. I met them, and they're very well behaved."

"Who are they, Debra?" asked Dad.

"They belong to the lady down the street—Mrs. Strickland. She and another lady, Mrs. Quinn, are coming to my neighborhood Bible study."

"What about—what was her name?—Mrs. Glover, the lady you talked to before?" Dad asked.

"Oh, she found a job right away. I've called on everyone, and Mrs. Quinn and Mrs. Strickland are the only ladies in the neighborhood without outside jobs. The only reason they're home is because they have babies or preschoolers."

Dad reached over and patted her hand. "I hope you're not having second thoughts about being a full-time wife and mother."

Mom smiled. "Of course not, dear. I chose this kind of life-style with my eyes wide open. I love it, wouldn't trade it for the world. But I'm afraid I must look like something of a failure in our neighbors' eyes."

"Well, in my eyes you're queen of the castle," said Dad with obvious pride.

"So when do I begin teaching these little kids?" asked Kasey.

"Whenever you wish, honey. Just give their mom a call."

"Well, I hope I'll be able to work them in," Kasey said with deliberate nonchalance. "I'm going to be pretty busy in the days ahead."

"Oh, you mean practicing for the piano contest," said Dad.

"Well, yes, that too," said Kasey, measuring her words with care as she glanced sideways at Keith. "The truth is, I'm seeing someone now, and he said he'll be giving me a call."

"Seeing someone?" echoed Keith dubiously. "Who are you seeing?"

"A boy. Someone you don't know," said Kasey loftily.

Dad set down his silverware. "You have a boyfriend, Kasey?"

Kasey backed down just a trifle. "Not exactly a boy-friend, Dad. At least not yet. Not officially. But he told a friend of mine he likes me. And—like I said—he promised to call."

# 9

Two weeks after Kasey's first visit to Shady Oaks, she joined Ryan and his friends for a second trip. This time Kasey managed to sit in the front seat of Ryan's car beside him. A dozen times during the drive Kasey considered mentioning Selena Hubbard and her many conversations with Ryan, but somehow she feared it would be a breach of the silence they had maintained so far about their relationship. She decided that it would be best to let Ryan bring up Selena's name first. If Ryan insisted on playing this little game of keeping their feelings for each other private, what could she do but go along with him? Certainly she would do nothing in the world to risk losing him now.

Besides, Kasey had never really gone with a boy before, so what did she know about the ground rules of steady dating? Although Ryan's secrecy seemed unusual, perhaps it was commonplace for guys not to want to make a big deal about having a girl friend. Whatever the case, Kasey sensed instinctively that she could trust Ryan. Any guy who was so considerate of the elderly would surely be gentle with her feelings.

As he drove, Ryan glanced over at Kasey and smiled. "I'm looking forward to hearing you play again, and so are the residents of Shady Oaks. They loved your playing last time."

"I'm glad," said Kasey shyly. "I thought this time I'd play the piece I'm working on for the all-school piano contest."

"Hey, that's terrific. I didn't know you'd entered the contest. But then, of course. You'd be a natural. I bet you'll win."

Kasey shook her head slowly. "I don't know. Laury Lassen is very good—"

"Sure, but so are you," said Ryan. "It'll be an exciting contest."

Kasey hadn't thought of it that way, but yes, she and Laury would make it an exciting program, a program the school could be proud of and the audience would enjoy. Somehow, Ryan's simple remark had helped her see the contest from a new perspective; the tight knot of anxieties she felt about competing with Laury was relaxing a little. How easily Ryan made her feel better. No wonder she was so crazy about him!

She realized suddenly that Ryan was saying something else to her, something about why no guys had come along for their visit to Shady Oaks.

"Sometimes it bums me out—their attitude, you know?"

"Their attitude?" she echoed, struggling to comprehend what he was saying.

"Yeah. Most guys are so worried about being macho, they think it's a sissy thing to go and visit old-timers at a retirement home. Some of 'em don't even bother to visit their own grandparents, so there's no getting through to them, you know? They don't realize how much it means to these people to get a little attention."

Kasey studied Ryan's handsome profile, the way his wavy brown hair curled over his forehead and the seriousness of his expression. "How come you care so much, Ryan?" she asked. "How come you're not like the other guys?"

He tossed her a jaunty little smile. "It's not that I'm so different from the other guys, Kasey. It's just that I got to see what it was like at Shady Oaks when my grandfather was there. Our family used to visit him a lot, but some of the people never had a single visitor. I could see them sitting there getting lonelier and lonelier every day. I vowed when Gramps died that I would go back and try to take a little happiness to the people there, sort of in Gramps's memory, you might say."

"You and your grandfather must have been very close."

He nodded. "I was the firstborn of five kids and the first grandchild, so I became Gramps's favorite. He was a fireman, and sometimes he'd take me to the station and let me sit in the big rigs or wear his fireman's hat or pretend I was holding one of the big hoses. Sometimes we'd sit in the station with the other men while they joked and laughed and swapped stories. I mean, I was in my glory. I thought I was big stuff."

Kasey chuckled. "I bet I know what you want to be— a fireman, right?"

Ryan laughed. "I once did, but not anymore. Now I'd like to do something to help people, maybe be a doctor or a therapist. I might even make geriatrics my specialty. Old folks need someone who understands their problems and can look out for their interests."

"I think that's a wonderful goal," said Kasey.

"Well, time will tell whether it's a pipe dream or not. If I can just keep my grades up and make it into medical school someday."

"Oh, you will, I know you will."

"How about you?" said Ryan. "What do you want to be?"

"A pianist."

"I should have known. What kind of music do you want to play?"

"Maybe classical. And inspirational. Like Dino. It's all I've ever dreamed of."

"Well, you've got the talent for it."

"I hope so. I really want to use my music for the Lord."

"Hey, are you two going to let anyone else get a word in edgewise?" said Nancy from the back seat.

Kasey's face flushed as she realized that she and Ryan had been so engrossed in conversation she had forgotten anyone else was in the car. "I'm sorry," she murmured. "I didn't mean to monopolize the—"

"Hey, I was kidding," said Nancy. "You two go ahead and talk. No problem."

"Well, we're here at Shady Oaks now," said Ryan as he pulled into the gravel driveway. "Everyone know what they're going to say?"

"You know us, Ryan," said Janice with a laugh. "We're old troupers by now. We've got our parts down pat."

"Great! And after our program we'll spend some time with the people just talking and listening, OK? Everyone pick out one or two people and get acquainted. Let them know you really care."

An hour later, as Kasey and Ryan and the others mingled with the residents of Shady Oaks, Kasey realized this was the best part of the evening. She liked meeting the people one by one and listening to their stories. It was amazing how many backgrounds were represented in this one little group.

Mrs. Smolin, the squat lady with a big smile and no teeth, claimed she had once been a cleaning lady in the White House. "I washed Mr. Roosevelt's laundry. Made sure he had the whitest shirts and handkerchiefs in all of Washington."

Mr. Suttles, the white-haired man who looked like Albert Einstein, had been a railroad engineer. "Trains today are like plastic toys compared to what we had forty years ago," he trumpeted in a gravelly voice filled with conviction. "Mark my words, young lady. Nothing can compare to the great Super Chief."

Mrs. Pinkelman, the pillow-shaped lady with the lace shawl and flowered hat, had performed in vaudeville. "I sang with George Burns before he met Gracie," she told Kasey as she absently twisted her pearl necklace around her index finger.

"I bet Mr. Burns was a handsome man back then," said Kasey.

"Yes, he was. Always had that twinkle in his eyes like he had a secret to tell. I was taken with him for months. Then Gracie came along." Mrs. Pinkelman's faded eyes grew wistful. "I still think he's the most handsome man I ever met."

After Kasey had spoken with several of the residents, she slipped over to Clarisa Huckabey's desk and asked, "Where's Mrs. Solomon this evening?"

Clarisa's forehead crinkled slightly. "Oh, it's the same as usual. When visitors come, she keeps to herself, stays in her room. She's a strange woman, remote, unapproachable. We've all tried to reach her, but without much success."

"Why?" asked Kasey. "Why is she so unfriendly?"

Clarisa lowered her voice. "No one knows for sure, but we think maybe she lost some relatives in the Holocaust. She won't speak of it, but if members of her family were imprisoned in the German concentration camps, that could sure account for her bitterness."

Kasey covered her mouth in horror. "No wonder she's so sad!"

Clarisa nodded. "Don't quote me, of course. Maybe I shouldn't even speculate. All I know for sure is that after the war Olive Solomon went on to become a famous opera star. But I imagine the poor woman carries around a load of anger and resentment over what happened to her family. No wonder she's a loner."

"I just wish she would let people get close to her," said Kasey. "Her life would be so much happier."

"Tell her that," said Clarisa dryly. "Around here, we've found that no one can tell Olive Solomon a thing."

Kasey shook her head sadly. "That's too bad, because I think she could use a friend. I think she's a very lonely lady."

Clarisa nodded. "True it is. But make no mistake, Kasey. They're all lonely here. Every one. Lonely."

On the way home that evening, as Ryan turned onto Kasey's street (she was the last to be dropped off this time!), she told him, "I'm going to figure out some way to get Mrs. Solomon out of her shell. I really want to make friends with her. Will you help me?"

Ryan shrugged. "Sure. But how? You got a plan?"

"No, not yet. But I'll think about it—and pray too. It won't help Mrs. Solomon to have friends if she doesn't find her very best Friend, the Lord Jesus."

Ryan looked over at Kasey and grinned. "Yeah, I found that out a long time ago."

"Me, too," she said. "I was five. In vacation Bible school. And Jesus has been my best Friend ever since."

"I was six," said Ryan. His voice turned thoughtful. "Do you realize that some of the people at Shady Oaks have lived eighty or ninety years and still don't understand that Jesus loves them?"

"We're trying to tell them," said Kasey.

Ryan nodded. "But why has it taken so many years for someone to tell them—or so many years for them to listen?"

# 10

In the final weeks before the Springfield High All-School Piano Competition, Kasey doubled her hours of practice each day. The more she played, the more confident she felt that she could win over Laury Lassen. Even though Laury was talented, her technique would surely suffer if she practiced as little as Keith had said.

Two weeks before the contest, Kasey learned there would be a special celebration party at the Springfield Hotel for the piano finalists and their families and friends. It would be held immediately after the competition to honor the winners and console the losers. Kasey's first thought was of Ryan. She simply had to invite him. And even though Selena said his mother frowned on her son's dating, surely she would make an exception for such a special occasion.

Still, Kasey found it hard to actually invite Ryan. Their relationship remained such a mystery to her. Their "dates" were confined to their occasional trips to the Shady Oaks Retirement Home, and always they were surrounded by others, so that there was no chance to talk privately.

How Kasey wanted to ask him about some of the things he had told Selena! And, why, she wondered, did Ryan insist on communicating with her only through Selena? Was he afraid of telling her personally how he felt? Was he afraid that they might get too serious or that she might expect some sort of commitment from him? Why did he insist on keeping their relationship on hold?

Again and again Kasey nearly blurted out to Ryan her countless questions about the strange nature of their relationship, about the secrecy of it all. But she always stopped herself, couldn't quite bring herself to say the words. According to Selena, Ryan had said this was the way things had to be. So why disrupt the fragile balance of something that meant so much to Kasey? Why risk inciting Ryan's anger or displeasure?

In spite of Kasey's doubts and questions, she was still determined to invite Ryan to the post-competition party at the Springfield Hotel. That special event might be just what she needed to give their relationship a little push.

On Monday morning, four days before the piano contest, Kasey decided this had to be the day she invited Ryan to the party. If she waited any longer he might have other plans. And, surely, the evening would not be complete without him there to cheer her on.

Even as Kasey entered homeroom that morning, she rehearsed in her mind what she would say to Ryan: *I've never complained about keeping our friendship low-key, Ryan, but this one time I need you with me. I want to be playing just for you.*

Kasey smiled inwardly as she slipped into her seat. How could Ryan possibly say no to such a request? He was the one who had encouraged her to compete, the one who had so often praised her playing at Shady Oaks. He was tied inextricably to the victory she knew would be hers.

Kasey's expectations about Ryan were buoyed even further when Selena sat down at her desk with a special twinkle in her eyes. Smugly she brushed her oily brown hair back from her face and drawled, "Guess what, Kasey?"

"What?" said Kasey, conscious of a sudden churning sensation in her stomach. When Selena used this particular voice it meant she had something important to say.

"I saw Ryan in the hall this morning, and you won't believe what he told me."

"What? Tell me! What?"

Selena lowered her voice to a whisper. "He wants to ask you to go around with him. I mean, I'm talking commitment here. He wants you to wear his class ring."

"You're kidding!"

"No, that's what he said. He said he appreciates your understanding that he can't make a big deal about liking you. I mean, if it ever got back to his mother—well, you know."

"But if his mother just knew me. If I could meet her—"

"Yeah, well, it's a bummer, all right. Anyway, he would love to give you his class ring, but he can't until he's a senior. His mother would have a fit, and he doesn't want to rock the boat right now."

"I understand," said Kasey in a small voice. "I don't mind. I don't need a ring."

Selena nodded breathlessly. "Well, he hoped you would understand. He's afraid you might not want to wait for him. Some girls are like that, you know."

"Not me," said Kasey earnestly. "I'd wait forever."

Selena smiled. "Yeah. That's what I figured." As the class bell rang, she slung her books under her arm and stood up. "See you after school. Our regular place, OK? I'll probably have some more news about Ryan."

Kasey nodded. She picked up her books and followed Selena out of the classroom. She didn't want to admit it, but sometimes she resented having to share Ryan with Selena. It was as if the three of them were bound together in this bizarre alliance, a safe, secret three-way connection that might go on indefinitely. Kasey wondered: Would her friendship with Selena even exist without Ryan? More important, could her friendship with Ryan exist without Selena? Such questions were too disquieting to think about now. She would concentrate instead on the fact that Ryan wanted her to be his steady girl.

At lunchtime Kasey couldn't resist sharing her latest news about Ryan with Jenny Clegg. Even as she spoke, she noticed that Laury Lassen's snobbish little coterie was sitting at the end of the table, so impulsively she raised her voice even more than she usually did for Jenny. "Ryan Dimarco wants me to wear his ring," she said, pronouncing each word precisely, "but we're going to wait until he's a senior."

Jenny moved her fingers, spelling out, "That's wonderful!" Then, in her softly rolling, gently cadent voice, she asked, "When did he ask you?"

Kasey glanced away uneasily. "He didn't exactly. Selena told me."

"Selena?" Jenny's smile toppled. "I don't understand."

"You know how it is," Kasey said with sudden impatience. She noticed that several of Laury's friends were watching and giggling. Was it because of what she'd said about Ryan? Or because she was talking with a deaf girl no one believed could speak? "I told you before, Jenny. Ryan and I are keeping things low-key. But someday—"

Jenny's fingers flew furiously.

"Wait," said Kasey. "I can't follow what you're saying—"

Jenny spoke the words slowly, with difficulty. "You must talk to Ryan. Make him tell you himself. Do not speak through Selena."

Kasey nodded. She'd known for a long time that it wasn't healthy to involve Selena so closely in her relationship with Ryan, but it had happened so gradually, so spontaneously. She felt safe speaking through Selena, not having to confront Ryan herself. It wouldn't be easy to change things. Selena might feel hurt if she were suddenly excluded.

Jenny reached out and shook Kasey's arm. With an odd urgency in her eyes, she said, "Do you understand what I am saying to you?"

Kasey blinked. "Yes, of course. And I'm going to take your advice. This very afternoon I'm asking Ryan to be my escort to the party Friday night to honor the piano contestants."

Jenny smiled. "Good. I am happy for you—and for Ryan."

In English class that afternoon, Kasey noticed that Ryan gave her an extra special smile. It spoke of all the promises and affection that could not be voiced aloud. Returning the smile, she felt warm and wonderful inside. It occurred to her that she should say something about the ring. Impulsively she leaned over and whispered, "I do understand about the ring, Ryan."

He looked puzzled. "The ring?"

"Yes. Your class ring. You know."

"Oh, yeah. Right," he murmured. "It's nice, isn't it?"

"Yes, it is," she said vaguely. Somehow he had missed what she was trying to say. She decided to try again. "Can I talk to you after class? I have something to ask you."

He smiled. "Sure. I'll meet you in the hall."

As the period drew to a close, Kasey's wrists began to tingle, and her mouth felt dry. She uttered a silent prayer that she would say just the right words to Ryan and that he would accept her invitation to the party. Then, as the class bell sounded and she gathered her books to leave, she felt a knot in the pit of her stomach. She started for the door, but her knees felt shaky too. It was certainly easier communicating with Ryan through Selena!

Ryan was waiting for her off to one side, a wry little smile on his lips. "I hope you're not going to tell me you can't make it to Shady Oaks next week. The people are crazy about your playing."

"No, that's not it," she said quickly. "I love going to Shady Oaks. Just let me know what time I should be ready."

"Yeah, sure. Great. I'll call you." He eyed her curiously. "So what did you want to talk to me about?"

She shifted her books nervously. "I—uh—I know you want to keep things kind of low-key—I mean, I understand about your mother and all—but I figured maybe just this once—"

Ryan shot her a frown of consternation. "My mother? What are you talking about—?"

Kasey's mouth felt like cotton as she babbled, "I'm sorry. I shouldn't have brought up your mother. What I really wanted to ask is—uh—could you go with me to the party after the piano competition Friday night?"

Ryan's smile returned. "Why, Kasey, I would love to—"

Her heart hammered wildly. "You would? Great!"

"Except—"

"Except—?" She could already feel her soaring spirits taking a nosedive.

He placed his hand lightly on her shoulder. "I wish you'd asked me sooner. I've already got a date."

"You do? But who—?"

"Laury Lassen."

Kasey's spirits crash-landed with a violent thud. "Laury? You're going with Laury?"

"Yeah. She and I are old friends. But that doesn't mean I won't be at the competition rooting you on too. I know you'll be fantastic."

Kasey shook her head as if to clear it. "I—I just don't understand, Ryan. After what you said this morning—"

"This morning? What do you mean? We didn't talk this morning, Kasey."

"No, not us. I mean Selena. After what you said to Selena this morning—"

He looked baffled. "Selena?"

"Yes. Selena. Selena Hubbard." A terrible, desperate pressure was rising in Kasey's chest. She felt feverish, confused. Her voice was pinched, shrill. "Why are you doing this, Ryan? You know Selena. She's a good friend of yours."

Ryan shook his head, bewildered. "I don't think I know her, Kasey. Oh, wait, is she a heavyset girl, kind of tall, with frizzy black hair?"

Kasey stared at him, open-mouthed. She felt as if a sudden paralysis were gripping her mind, her body. She felt too limp to nod, but Ryan continued without seeming to notice. "I think she works in the cafeteria with me fifth period. She's kind of a loner, keeps to herself—? Is she the one you mean, Kasey?"

This time Kasey forced a nod. "But you—you don't talk to each other?"

"Oh, I guess we've said a few words once or twice. Hi—how are you?—great day—that sort of thing. But I

67

can't say we've ever had a real conversation. Why do you ask?''

Over the stunned disappointment sweeping her heart and mind, Kasey managed to say, "It's not important, Ryan. I shouldn't have said anything. Forget what I said.''

He stared questioningly at her for a moment, then grinned pleasantly. "Whatever you say, Kasey. Anyway, I'm sorry Laury beat you to the punch for Friday night. Come over and say hi to us at the party, OK?" He squeezed her arm in an almost comradely gesture. "Actually, you and Laury have a lot in common. It'd be cool for you two to get better acquainted.''

"Uh, I don't know. Maybe," Kasey whispered, looking away, biting her lip to keep back the tears. "I—uh—I gotta go. I gotta get home. 'Bye, Ryan.''

She turned and ran down the hall, darting around passing classmates, her heels clicking noisily on the tile floor. Everything around her—the metal lockers, classroom doors, posters on the wall—blurred and swayed and seemed suddenly foreign and meaningless. Her glasses were clouded with the moisture of her tears. She whisked them off and stuck them in her coat pocket.

She walked in a slow, even stride now, moving as if in a trance. She could hear the sounds around her, but they seemed to come from a distance. They did not touch her. Boys shouted to one another, lockers slammed, coats rustled, a dozen voices blended into one continuous, dull sound moving heavily on the air, like something ominous, threatening.

Kasey gazed ahead, transfixed by the shimmering, pastel haze of her private, nearsighted world. The long bleak hallway seemed like an endless tunnel. She shivered, feeling suddenly cold and dark and frail inside. She might blow away like a leaf. She might crumble like a ball

68

of clay. She could disappear from the earth, and no one would know the difference. Nothing would be affected. In fact, disappearing might be a good thing. Then no one would guess what a terrible incredible fool she had made of herself.

# 11

There was no reason for Kasey to wait for Selena tonight, but she waited anyway, out of habit, just outside Springfield High's main double doors. It was snowing, not the first snow of the season, but almost, and there was a fine white coat like lamb's wool covering the lawn, the sidewalks, the streets. Everything was blinding white, with the frosty sheen of faded sunlight glinting off a fantasyland of snowflakes and ice crystals.

Kasey squinted at the passers-by, but without her glasses the faces and figures were a bright, anonymous blur, like the hazy, unfinished forms in impressionistic paintings.

Then, after a few moments, Selena appeared, pulling her coat collar up around her neck and shrieking something about the dizzying maze of snow flurries.

Kasey stared at Selena's round, pink, blank face, but she couldn't quite distinguish Selena's features. The heavy brows were simply smudge marks, her eyes beady exclamation points, and her usual prickly wreath of coal-black hair could have been a cloud of smoke hovering uncertainly around her head.

"Where are your glasses?" Selena asked.

"In my pocket," said Kasey.

"Well, put them on. You're squinting like an owl."

"I can't. They're dirty."

"Then how will you see to get home?"

"It doesn't matter," said Kasey.

"What do you mean?" Selena probed. "What's wrong with you?"

"Nothing. Everything," said Kasey, her voice wavering.

"Well, then let's go. I've got lots to tell you."

"What?"

"What do you think? About Ryan. What else?"

Kasey forced her voice to remain steady, but it still came out uneven, unnaturally breathless. "Did you ever stop to think, Selena—it's funny, but we—we never talk about anything but Ryan."

"So? What else is there to talk about? I mean, that's what you want, isn't it?"

"Yes, I guess it is." Kasey swallowed a rising sob. She could feel the tears welling in her eyes. She blinked, trying to force them back. "You knew how much I cared about him, Selena—"

"Yeah, sure. You're totally in love. It's great. And wait'll you hear what Ryan said today. You won't believe this, Kasey—"

Kasey turned away as the tears spilled down her cold cheeks. She wondered if the salty drops might freeze on her face like miniature crystal balls.

"Kasey, did you hear me?" Selena urged. Her breath came out in opaque little clouds of air. "I was saying—telling you—Ryan was so glad you understood about the ring—"

Kasey started down the snowy steps.

Selena followed. "Are you listening, Kasey? I said, you won't believe—"

Kasey pivoted and stared hard at Selena. "You're right. I won't believe. Not anymore. I know better."

Selena's mouth gaped in bewilderment. "What's wrong, Kasey? You sound upset. You're not mad at me, are you?"

At last the floodgates opened. Kasey couldn't hold anything back. "Why did you do it?" she screamed, her voice rising shrilly on the thin, icy air. "Why did you lie? You didn't even know him! Why, Selena, why?"

For a moment Selena's expression remained blank, baffled; then a look of sudden comprehension swept over her features, and she said, "Oh, you found out."

"You said he was your friend," Kasey rushed on, her voice sodden with anguish. "You said he liked me. But he never told you anything, did he? You made it all up!"

Selena cleared her throat uneasily. "It was a game, that's all; just a game."

"But why, Selena? Why would you want to hurt me like that?"

Selena shrugged. "I didn't want to hurt you, Kasey. It just happened. I never thought it would go so far, but you—you hung on every word I said. I never dreamed you'd believe everything."

Kasey brushed at her tears. "But I did believe you! I did!"

"Because you wanted to," argued Selena.

"How could I be so totally stupid—?"

Selena nodded. "Yeah. I know. I didn't think anybody in the world could be so gullible, but there you were."

Kasey shook her head, dazed. Selena looked vague, unreal, her features fuzzy, not quite there. Kasey had a hard time focusing on her face. Was there any remorse in Selena's expression, any regret? "It was all some hideous joke, wasn't it, Selena?" Kasey said bitterly. "Just you and me and a pack of lies. Ryan didn't know a thing about our so-called relationship. He never cared about me—"

"That's not true," said Selena. "You've made friends with him. Maybe he does care—"

"If he cared," shrieked Kasey, "he wouldn't be dating Laury Lassen Friday night!"

Selena stared quizzically at Kasey. "He's dating Laury Lassen? Oh, wow! Listen, Kasey, I had no idea." She gave Kasey's shoulder a sympathetic squeeze. "Come on. We'll talk on the way home."

Kasey jerked away. "Don't you get it, Selena? I don't want to see you again. I don't want to see anyone! I just want to die!"

"No, Kasey! Wait! Don't—!"

Kasey broke into a run, her books bouncing crazily in her arms, her feet slipping on the snowy wet sidewalk. With an ache in her chest that nearly stopped her breath, she ran blindly, leaping from the curb into the street, propelled by a sudden nameless energy that dazed her senses.

When she heard Selena shout her name, Kasey reacted instinctively, stopping abruptly in midair. It seemed that she had been caught momentarily on slow-motion film or in a freeze-frame of videotape, that the cessation of movement had left her hanging in space, trapped for an instant in a gesture of reversing herself.

A sleek automobile screamed by like a bullet spraying her with fresh snow and slush. Kasey squinted after it in astonishment, comprehending that in another moment she would have been slammed under its roaring wheels. She turned to see Selena running toward her.

"Are you all right, Kasey?" Selena panted, her bulky frame bending forward, her face full of concern.

Kasey stepped shakily back onto the slick sidewalk. A shiver traveled the full length of her spine. "Uh, yes, I think so," she uttered thinly. "When you screamed, I knew something was wrong."

"You would have run right out in front of that car," Selena cried breathlessly. "What were you trying to do? Kill yourself?"

Kasey shook her head. She felt confused and weak and a little sick to her stomach. "I didn't see the car. Without my glasses I couldn't see anything."

Selena sighed in relief. "I thought maybe what you said about wanting to die—"

"No, I didn't mean that. I was wrong to say it. I don't want to die. I just—" The tears started again, fresh and salty and warm on her icy cheeks. "I just want to go home, Selena. Please go away. Leave me alone. Just let me go home and hide."

# 12

Kasey headed for bed early that evening, excusing herself from dinner because her stomach felt queasy and, as she told her mother, for some strange reason she just wasn't hungry.

"Maybe I picked up a bug or something," she said lamely, escaping from the table and her parents' questioning glances.

"Hey, Sis, don't tell me you've already got the jitters over the piano contest on Friday," said Keith as she darted toward the stairs.

She felt too drained and exhausted even to try for a suitable comeback. Once alone in her room, she locked the door, undressed quickly, and pulled on her warm, flannel pajamas. She slipped a Dino cassette into her tape deck, turning the volume down almost to a whisper. Then she gathered up her stuffed Winnie the Pooh she'd cherished since kindergarten and curled up in the rocking chair by the window. She cuddled the floppy old bear and kissed its worn, nubby head. She gazed somberly out the window at the softly falling snow and let her tears flow once again.

When her tears were finally spent and her Kleenex box nearly empty, Kasey dried her eyes and spoke aloud over the massive lump in her throat. "Dear Lord Jesus," she said haltingly, "I haven't talked to You as much since we came here to Springfield. I don't know why that is. I'm lonelier here. And sadder. And I need You more than I ever did. I thought things were finally going to work out in this town, but now I know I was wrong about everything. I won't ever fit in. I won't ever have friends like I had in Middleton. In fact, now I feel too humiliated to even show my face at school.

"Dear God, why did You let me make such a fool of myself? How could You let me be so dumb? I really believed Ryan liked me. I thought everything in my life was turning out just perfect. How could I have been so wrong?"

She was silent for a minute, waiting, as if she expected God to somehow explain Himself or apologize for messing up her life. But, as she thought about it—underneath the overwhelming ache—she knew that God was still in charge; He knew exactly what He was doing. Hadn't He said in His Word that He would work all things for her good?

She mulled it over. Actually, the verse said, "And we know that all things work together for good to them that love God, to them who are the called according to his purpose." Did she really love God? Or did she love what God could do for her? Was she one of the "called"? Called to do what? And what did the words mean "according to his purpose"? What was God's purpose for her, for a plain, foolish, unhappy girl named Kasey Carlone?

"Dear Jesus, I know I should ask You to forgive me for my lousy attitude," she said quietly, "but right now I just feel like complaining and feeling miserable. I hope You'll understand."

The next morning at breakfast Kasey told her mother that she didn't feel well enough to go to school.

"I hope you're not coming down with that awful strain of flu that's going around this winter."

"No, Mom," said Kasey, dawdling idly with her oatmeal, "I think I just need a few days of rest here at home."

Her mother gave her a quizzical glance. "All right, hon, go back to bed. But we'll talk about this later, OK? After I get Dad off to work and Keith off to school."

An hour later Kasey's mother came to her room and sat down on the edge of Kasey's bed. "Feeling any better?" she asked, placing a cool hand on her forehead.

"Not really," said Kasey, avoiding her mother's gaze.

"You don't have a fever. I think it's something else, maybe something not physical at all. Care to talk about it, honey?"

Kasey had vowed to carry the secret of her terrible stupidity and humiliation to the grave, but hearing the warm, confidential tone in her mother's voice prompted a fresh onslaught of tears. Before she knew it, she was pouring out the entire story of Selena's deception and her own incredible gullibility. She finished with, "How could I have been so naive, Mom? How could I have let it go on for weeks and weeks without knowing she was lying to me?"

"Perhaps because you wanted so much for it to be true."

"But when I think back on it now, I realize how impossible it all was. It's so clear now. How could I have been so blind? How could I have been such an idiot?"

Her mother moved over beside Kasey and gently massaged her neck. "You believed Selena because you assume everyone is as honest and sincere as you are. That's not bad, honey. That means you can see the good in people that others sometimes miss, and it means that people can always trust you to be open and straight with them."

Kasey folded her arms across her chest. "And here I thought Selena Hubbard was my friend. And all this time she was laughing behind my back!"

"Maybe not," said Mom. "Maybe she wanted to be your friend and just didn't know how, so she did what she thought would please you."

Kasey wrinkled her nose. "Friends don't lie like that, Mom."

"Well, then, what about you, Kasey? Were you Selena's friend?"

Kasey stared quizzically at her mother. "Of course! We talked together every day, ate lunch together sometimes, walked home from school together every night. I trusted her, Mom!"

"That's not what I mean, Kasey. I mean, how much did you find out about Selena? Is she a Christian? What's her home life like? What does she want to do with her life?"

Kasey thought a moment. "Hm, I don't know. We mainly just talked about Ryan."

"Then do you see what was happening, Kasey? Maybe you were using Selena as much as she was using you. She wanted a friend, someone who would make her feel important. You wanted someone to help you get close to Ryan. So maybe Selena isn't completely to blame for what happened."

Kasey chewed on her lower lip for a moment, then looked up sheepishly at her mother. "You're saying I should forgive Selena? I should forget everything that happened?"

"I'm saying, instead of concentrating on your own distress, maybe you should try being a real friend to Selena. Who knows? She might really blossom with a little kindness and attention."

Kasey removed her glasses and cleaned the lenses on a corner of the sheet. "Really, Mom! You mean I should befriend Selena like I'm trying to befriend the old folks at Shady Oaks?"

"Yes. And like you're doing with the neighborhood youngsters who come here for piano lessons each week. That's your gift, Kasey. Making people feel loved. It's a very rare and special gift."

Kasey smiled tolerantly at her mother. "Sure, Mom. That's the sort of thing you tell someone who's only average at everything else or who has no outstanding talent. But God did give me a talent to play the piano, and that's what I want to do best for Him."

Her mother stood up and smiled. "Well, in that case, maybe you'd better get ready and head for school. You've got a lot to do before the piano competition on Friday night."

# 13

For two days Kasey couldn't bring herself to speak to Selena Hubbard. Selena, in turn, avoided all eye contact with Kasey. Finally, in homeroom on Thursday, Kasey said in a low, even voice, "Will you meet me after school, Selena? I think we should talk."

They walked home in a light snowfall even though Keith had offered to drive them. After covering several blocks in silence, Kasey said, "Listen, Selena, I know we should talk, but honestly, I don't even know what to say to you."

Selena shuffled along in an awkward gait. "I guess you're still pretty mad, huh?"

"Mad? Yeah, that's one of the things I'm feeling." Kasey kept her eyes straight ahead. The snow flurries made feathery little marks on her glasses. "But I'm feeling lots of other things too."

"Like what?"

"Like, I'm angry, and hurt. And ashamed that I was such a fool. But I feel sorry too."

"Sorry? You mean for what I did to you—lying about Ryan?"

"That too. But I also feel sorry for not being a better friend to you, Selena."

Selena's forehead wrinkled in perplexity. "Is this a riddle or something, Kasey, or are you trying to make me feel worse than I already feel?"

"No, I'm not. It's just that my mom made me realize I wasn't being much of a friend either. I was more interested in finding out about Ryan than in getting acquainted with you."

Selena managed a crooked little smile. "Does this mean all is forgiven? We can be friends after all?"

"I want to try," said Kasey. "I can't promise—you know—that we'll be buddy-buddy or anything. It's hard. I can't change my feelings by myself, but I know Jesus can help me if I ask Him."

Selena's thick brows arched curiously. "Jesus?"

"Yes." Kasey gathered her words carefully. "He's my best Friend, Selena. He loves me even though I don't deserve His love, and He forgives me when I tell Him I'm sorry for doing things wrong. That's what true friendship is, Selena. I want to try to follow His example and be your friend."

Selena shook her head, baffled. "You blow my mind, Kasey. I never heard anyone talk like that. You know, you're really OK."

"It's not me," said Kasey. "It's Jesus. He's the special One. If you really want a wonderful friend, He's the One to have."

Selena grinned and said lightly, "You think so? Well, who knows? Maybe sometime you can make the introductions."

Kasey smiled. "Just watch. I'm going to take you up on that, Selena."

That evening, as Kasey spent her final hours in practice for the piano competition, she was still thinking about Selena and how she had almost missed an opportunity to tell her about Jesus. Speaking to others about her faith wasn't something Kasey thought about every day. In fact, it sure didn't come naturally. Sometimes days and even weeks went by before she remembered that many people didn't have Jesus to turn to with their problems. They didn't know He wanted to be their Savior and Friend. People like Selena, and Olive Solomon, and even Laury Lassen. Why was it so much easier to be concerned about winning piano competitions and having a boyfriend than whether people knew Jesus?

When Kasey arrived in homeroom on Friday, she was glad she had resolved things with Selena. Now if only she could feel at ease with Ryan. But all week she had felt awkward and tongue-tied around him. Thankfully, he knew nothing about Kasey's foolish assumption that he considered her his girl friend. And at least they were still friends. They would spend time together occasionally at Shady Oaks. She would also see Ryan tonight at the piano competition and celebration party, but, of course, he would be with Laury Lassen.

In fact, Laury Lassen was the first person Kasey encountered when she arrived backstage for the contest that evening. Laury was chatting casually with two other contestants. They were making jokes about something—Kasey couldn't hear their words, but she heard the light, echoing ring of Laury's laughter. Kasey stood off to one side clutching her music, wondering whether to go over and intrude on the conversation or keep her distance and risk appearing rude. Finally she walked over and offered a tentative, "Hi."

Laury gave her a withering glance and uttered an icy, "Why, hello, Kasey. What a surprise to see you here. You must have been absolutely thrilled to qualify for this contest."

Kasey nodded. "Yes, but I've worked hard to earn that right."

Laury rolled her eyes heavenward. "Oh, I think that is so admirable, Kasey. Every day I told myself I just had to practice, but then something—or someone—would come along and distract me. I guess I'm just going to have to depend on mere talent."

One of the other contestants, a blonde named Judy something, shook her head and exclaimed, "Can you believe it? This girl doesn't even practice, and what do you wanna bet she walks away with top honors?"

Laury merely shrugged and pranced away with her chin held high.

Kasey watched her with a mixture of resentment and envy. How could Laury take so lightly a contest Kasey faced with fear and trembling? "She's either a fool or a fake," Kasey murmured under her breath.

Suddenly the music instructors were signaling that it was time to begin. Kasey's palms began to perspire, and her pulse raced. At least she was one of the first contestants scheduled to perform, so she could finish her piece, then relax and enjoy the rest of the program.

The contestants remained backstage until their names were called one by one. Kasey listened carefully as the first two played their pieces. They did well, but their selections were routine. The field was still wide open.

Then, as if in a dream, Kasey heard her name over the loudspeaker. "Ladies and gentlemen, Miss Kassandra Carlone, playing the First Movement of the "Sonata quasi una Fantasia," or *Moonlight Sonata*, by Ludwig van Beethoven."

Trancelike, Kasey walked out onto the stage, her shoulders squared, her head held high. She sat down at the beautiful old Steinway and carefully placed her music. A pause, then she began the sonata, *adagio sostenuto*. Her long, slender fingers moved deftly over the keys, the music swelling, swelling, filling the huge auditorium. She imagined her friend Jenny Clegg, with her palms pressed against the polished veneer, feeling the vibrations, saying, *Yes, it is like a rolling river, a surging ocean, an eagle in flight, rain on the windowpane* . . .

And then it was done, and she was standing, bowing amid wonderful waves of applause. She had done well. She sensed it, felt the warmth and approval of the audience. They liked her. She had pleased them. She felt euphoric, deliriously, deliciously in sync with God and mankind and the universe. She would win the piano competition; she knew it. She had lived all her life for this night!

Now it was Laury's turn. The announcer boomed, "Ladies and gentlemen, Miss Laury Lassen, playing Richard Addinsell's 'Warsaw Concerto.'"

Kasey was prepared not to like Laury's performance. Surely it would be sloppy, perhaps even embarrassing. No amount of talent could make up for the long, laborious hours of daily practice.

She listened with a critical ear to the first lively stanzas. Amazingly, they were impressive. And incredibly, Laury's timing and technique were flawless. Kasey held her breath lest she miss even a measure of the powerful, spirited concerto. Was it possible? Laury was playing to perfection. Not a missed beat or a wrong note in the entire piece. And she played with the high drama and polish of a seasoned performer!

As the final notes of the concerto reverberated in the hushed auditorium, Kasey's hopes for first place vanished with them. The audience was ecstatic, the applause deafening. Kasey knew even before the others played that the blue ribbon belonged to Laury Lassen.

# 14

Just as Kasey expected, Laury Lassen won first place in the Springfield All-School Piano Competition. At least Kasey was consoled by the fact that she took second place. At the celebration party in the Starlight Ballroom of the Springfield Hotel, Kasey's parents, friends, and teachers hugged her and praised her.

But the main attention was focused on Laury Lassen, who somehow managed to make a media event of her victory. Reporters from the local radio and television stations and the *Springfield News* swarmed around her, their cameras rolling and flashbulbs popping while Laury preened and posed for her adoring public.

"Well, she's in her glory," Keith murmured to Kasey. "After all this fanfare, she'll never give me the time of day."

"I thought you didn't care, brother dear," mused Kasey, "what with the bevy of beauties always surrounding you."

"I don't care—much. But you gotta admit she's something else. Talk about class and style!"

Kasey glanced over at Laury as she flitted about like a princess before her court, tittering gaily, bestowing benevolent smiles upon anyone who caught her eye. "She acts like she was born to win." Kasey sighed, trying without success to stifle her envy.

Keith nodded admiringly. "Yeah, she's the sort of girl who's just naturally meant to be on top. First rate."

Kasey winced inwardly. She wanted to turn the question back to Keith: *Who am I? A girl who was meant to fail?*

But she bit her lip to silence herself. She hadn't failed. She had won second place. She was better than all the other contestants—except for one. She was almost the best. Almost, but not quite. Why did that fact hurt so much? Why couldn't she be satisfied with second place?

Suddenly, a deep, familiar voice broke into her reverie. She turned with a start and looked up into the warm, approving eyes of Ryan Dimarco. "Hi, Ryan," she murmured shyly.

"Hi, Kasey," he said, placing his hands squarely on her shoulders. "Congratulations, my friend. You were terrific tonight. Just as I knew you'd be."

"Th—Thank you, Ryan. I'm glad you liked it."

"I just wish our friends from Shady Oaks could have heard you."

"Me too, but then they hear me play almost every week."

"Not nearly enough," said Ryan. "You're really a natural."

Before Kasey could respond, a lilting, singsong voice broke into the conversation with, "Yes, you played very nicely, Kasey."

Kasey glanced around as Laury Lassen sidled up to Ryan and took his arm possessively. "Yes, indeed," Laury continued in her most honey-coated tone, "you surprised us all, Kasey—or is it Kassandra? No, 'Kassandra' sounds much too sophisticated. 'Kasey' fits you so much better. It's so plain and simple and down to earth."

"Congratulations, Laury," Kasey said evenly, holding her temper. "You played beautifully."

Laury laughed lightly. "Yes, I was pleased, considering what little time I spend at the piano. My instructor keeps telling me if I practiced there's no telling what I could do. Maybe one of these days I'll find out."

"Do you want a professional career in music?" asked Kasey politely, making conversation. "Or is music just a diversion for you?"

Laury snuggled close to Ryan and purred, "A diversion? Certainly. A career? Well, maybe, maybe not. It depends on whether a better offer comes along."

Ryan chuckled good-naturedly. "Come on, Laury. You know you've dreamed about studying piano at Juilliard since you were old enough to reach the pedals."

She made a pouty little face. "Ryan knows me too well. We go back almost forever, don't we, Ryan? He's always been there for me."

"Our parents were friends before we were born," Ryan told Kasey offhandedly. "So Laury and I practically grew up together."

"And now we have a wonderful evening planned," said Laury plaintively, "so if you'll excuse us, Kasey?"

"Sure. So long, Ryan. Congratulations again, Laury."

Ryan paused and looked back. "Hey, Kasey, how about Sunday afternoon for Shady Oaks? Around two?"

"Yeah, sure, that sounds great. See you then."

On Sunday afternoon Kasey paced the floor as she waited for Ryan. This would be their first time together since she learned of Selena's lies. The truth still hurt keenly—the fact that Ryan considered her only a friend, nothing more. The lovely fantasy world Kasey had imagined for Ryan and herself had burst like a tiny, incandescent soap bubble. Now she must face him knowing there would never be anything more than friendship between them. But if there was any consolation, it was that Ryan didn't know what a fool she had made of herself.

Ryan was his usual cheerful self when she finally greeted him at the door. "It's cold out," he said, shivering in his bulky parka, "so bundle up in your warmest coat."

Minutes later, as Ryan drove down Wildwood Street toward the intersection, Kasey looked over at him and asked, "So who do we pick up first?"

"Nobody," he said with a smile. "I have some ideas about Shady Oaks I'd like to kick around with you first."

"With me?"

"Yeah. Besides myself, I think you're the most committed to really helping the people there."

"Well, yes, if I can, but I don't know what—"

"Just wait. I'll tell you my plan." He flipped on his turn signal. "You like hamburgers?"

"Of course, but—"

"I figured we could talk over a hamburger and fries," he said as he swung into a Big Boy's parking lot. "I hope you're hungry."

"Starved!" she cried, dismissing the fact that she'd just finished dinner.

Later, as they sat in a back corner booth leisurely dipping French fries into catsup, Ryan said, "You know, it's almost Christmas, and I've been trying to think of something special we could do for the folks at Shady Oaks."

"You mean like take them Christmas presents?"

"Yeah, or turkeys and pies and stuff for a fancy dinner."

"I think that's a wonderful idea! And what if we went out and chopped down a huge Christmas tree and took it in and decorated it for them?"

Ryan grinned. "Maybe we can talk the principal into making Shady Oaks an official school project. Think he'd go for the idea?"

"Sure! Why not? We could ask all the students to bring canned goods and treats and stuff. Or maybe little wrapped gifts—"

"Terrific!" said Ryan. "Practical little gifts they could use, like hand cream and stationery and large-print books and socks—"

Kasey shook her head in amazement. "Ryan, how do you know all these things—what the people need—what makes them happy—?"

He smiled wistfully. "My grandfather, remember? The few people who used to visit him always brought candy and flowers. Well, the flowers died, and Gramps couldn't eat the candy. What he really needed were warm socks, and slippers with rubber soles, and a magnifying glass so he could read the newspaper—" He paused and stared down silently at his plate for a moment.

Kasey said quietly, "You really miss him, don't you?"

Ryan blinked and looked away. "It still shows, huh?"

"It's nice," said Kasey. "I never knew a guy who cared so much about other people."

Ryan's face reddened slightly. "Well, I'm not trying out for any halo, if that's what you think. I probably wouldn't be any different than the next guy if it weren't for Gramps."

Kasey smiled. "I think you would be."

Ryan was silent again.

"Is something wrong?" asked Kasey. "You look so serious."

He glanced up and managed a crooked little smile. "Yeah, there is something, Kasey. I just don't know how to get into it."

"A problem?"

"I don't know. It's more puzzling than anything, I guess."

"I—I don't understand."

Ryan's facial muscles tightened. "It's about you, Kasey."

"Me?"

He nodded. "Something I heard. It doesn't make any sense."

Kasey felt a sudden wave of panic sweep over her. Her mouth felt dry as sandpaper. In a small, pinched voice, she asked, "What did you hear?"

"It's—well, this is kind of embarrassing—uh, especially if someone was just pulling my leg—" He shifted uneasily. "Listen, Kasey, if I'm way off base, just tell me. But someone told me you were—they said you were telling kids around school that we—you and I—were going around together—and that I wanted to give you my class ring." He rubbed his hand across his mouth and looked away. "Man, this is crazy. I can't believe I'm saying this to someone like you. There's gotta be some mistake somewhere—"

Tears welled in Kasey's eyes. She blinked them back, but they spilled over anyway.

Ryan studied her with a fierce intensity. "Kasey, are you—you're not crying, are you? Come on, it's not true, is it? You didn't tell people that we're—?"

"Yes." She lowered her head and covered her face with her hands. "Yes, I did."

"But why?"

She shook her head in despair. "It's a long story, Ryan. I never wanted you to know."

"I can't believe it, Kasey." He raked his fingers through his mop of thick brown hair. "I know you. You wouldn't lie like that—"

Kasey quickly brushed away her tears. "You found out from Laury, didn't you? She told you."

"Well, yeah, I did. Some of her friends overheard you telling someone else. I told her she was crazy, but she insisted it was true." He shook his head in bewilderment. "I just don't get it, Kasey. Why would you do it?"

She lowered her gaze and whispered haltingly, "Because—because I believed it was true."

Ryan stared at her. "You believed that—you and I—?"

"Can we talk about it privately, Ryan? Really, I'll tell you the whole story. But not here. Please."

He reached for the check. "OK, sure. We'll talk in the car on our way to Shady Oaks."

As Ryan drove through Springfield's snow-cloaked streets, Kasey poured out all the painful, humiliating details of Selena's deception. "I believed everything she told me about you, Ryan. I know it sounds totally dumb, but that's the honest truth. So you see, I really believed every word Laury's friends heard me say."

Ryan pulled into the driveway at Shady Oaks and turned off the engine. He sat for a long minute staring straight ahead, his face expressionless as he drummed his fingers absently on the dashboard.

"Please, say something, Ryan," Kasey begged. "Please understand. Don't be angry with me."

He shifted in his seat and gazed directly at her. "Angry? I'm not angry, Kasey. Is that what you thought—that I'd be mad at you?"

"Yes, of course. I—I embarrassed you. And made a fool of myself. I never wanted you to find out."

He reached over and tilted her chin toward him. "Kasey, listen to me. Why would I be angry? I—I'm flattered."

"Flattered?"

"Yes. I had no idea you felt that way about me. It just never occurred to me that you—well, you know. This changes everything."

Kasey nodded sadly. "I'll understand if you decide we shouldn't see each other—I mean, at Shady Oaks and all. I know how you feel about Laury—"

"Laury? You think Laury and I have something going?"

Kasey searched Ryan's face. He looked amused. "Don't you?"

"No way. Laury's not my type. I mean, she's a good friend, but she's totally off the wall. I could never deal with all her hangups." Ryan sighed deeply. "And, most important, Laury's not a Christian. I've talked to her, prayed for her, but she's just not interested." Ryan gently touched Kasey's chin. "Don't you see? Laury would never enjoy spending time with the folks at Shady Oaks. She'd never get a kick out of helping people or listening to their problems. That's the beautiful thing about you, Kasey. That's what I love about you."

Kasey stared at Ryan in spellbound astonishment. Had she heard right? Or had she been hypnotized by her own moonstruck fantasies? Then, before she could utter a word, the answer came as Ryan leaned over, removed her glasses, and kissed her lightly on the lips.

# 15

In the days that followed Kasey's special Sunday afternoon with Ryan, one thought rang over and over in her mind: Ryan liked her! Was it possible? The idea was awesome. But yes, it was a fact. He had said so. And he had kissed her, once, ever so gently. Their relationship would never be the same, for it was touched now by a spark of magic, the heady fragrance of romance.

Not that Kasey and Ryan were officially going around together or had made an actual commitment. But things were different now, subtly, wonderfully different. There was a special light in Ryan's eyes when he looked at her, a special lilt in his voice when they talked.

Kasey felt as if she were walking two feet above the ground. She possessed a joyous secret: Ryan Dimarco cared for her, was actually attracted to her! Even though Laury Lassen had won the piano competition, Kasey felt a new confidence inside, a sense that she could be a winner too someday, if she persevered enough. Hadn't she won out over Laury for Ryan's heart? If she could win Ryan, then anything was possible.

It was this new self-confidence that prompted Kasey to enter the prestigious Springfield City Piano Competition. With brimming excitement, she told Ryan about it when he picked her up on Saturday for some Christmas shopping at the local K-Mart.

"Would you believe, Ryan, that my piano teacher recommended me for the contest? You can't even enter without a teacher's recommendation. He thinks I could actually win—me, Kasey Carlone! Can you imagine what it would mean?"

"Whoa! Hold on. Give me the facts here." Ryan laughed as they walked from the congested parking lot toward the sprawling store.

"Oh, Ryan, it's totally awesome," she cried breathlessly. "The Springfield contest is part of the national Mozart Competition. It's incredibly famous."

"Famous, huh?" He followed her through the automatic doors into a maze of buzzing humanity. Christmas wreaths, giant Santas, and garlands of mistletoe decorated every aisle, while "Silent Night" wafted from the loudspeaker. "You're saying this contest is the Big Time for you?" said Ryan, speaking over the din.

"Right." Kasey fell into step beside him. He swung his arm lightly around her shoulder as she continued excitedly. "You see, every year cities across the country hold preliminaries. That's what I'll be entering. Then the winner in each city is sent to the state finals, and those winners compete in the national contest—"

"That's terrific, Kasey." He guided her through the bustling, jostling crowd to the notions department. "So when's the big day?"

"The contest isn't until March—and that's good, because I've got a ton of practicing to do! I'll have to work harder than I've ever worked in my life, but it'll be worth it."

"So what do you win—a blue ribbon, a trophy—?"

Kasey laughed. "No way, Ryan. If I win the Springfield Competition, I'll receive—listen to this!—a five-thousand dollar scholarship to the music school of my choice."

He grinned. "Hey, we're talking big bucks!"

She leaned her face close to his. "And if I win the state finals, it's twenty-five thousand dollars."

"And the national contest?"

"A full scholarship to the Juilliard School of Music, or the school of my choice!"

"Not bad," said Ryan approvingly. "That's quite an incentive."

She nodded. "It's what I've always dreamed of—being the best at something, not just average at everything. I want to do it for the Lord, too, Ryan—to let people know that Christians can be successful, that God will help us do our best. Don't you think if I won, it would be a great testimony to others?"

"Yeah. As Christians, we should try to be the best at whatever we do." He nudged her teasingly. "I know I'm the best at wolfing down cheeseburgers. Wanna hit Big Boy's when we're through here?"

She smiled. "If you promise we can split a chocolate shake."

They spent nearly two hours at K-Mart selecting inexpensive gifts for their many friends at Shady Oaks. Then, after their burgers at Big Boy's, they headed for Ryan's house. "I told the gang at school and church to meet at my place at seven so we can wrap these gifts for Shady Oaks. We'll see how many show up."

"They better show," said Kasey, "or we'll need Santa and all his elves to get ready for our Christmas party tomorrow."

"My dad will take the tree over to Shady Oaks in his pickup," said Ryan. "Nancy and Janice will bring the food we collected, and we'll take the presents."

"Would you believe, Clarisa has had the residents making their own ornaments all week long," said Kasey, "but she didn't tell them we're bringing a real tree."

Ryan grinned. "I can't wait to see their faces when we come marching in with that giant spruce and all this loot."

"It'll be the best Christmas ever," said Kasey.

"For them, you mean?"

"For all of us!"

The next morning, right after church, Ryan picked up Kasey and they drove to Shady Oaks with their trunkload of gifts. Minutes later Ryan's father pulled up in his old pickup with a giant blue spruce. Amid countless exclamations of surprise and joy, father and son carried the huge tree inside and set it up in the far corner by the window. Watching this Yuletide ritual, the old folks of Shady Oaks broke into vigorous applause.

Nancy and Janice and a dozen other high-schoolers arrived then with armloads of groceries—frozen turkeys, fresh fruits and vegetables, bread and cereal, and canned goods galore.

" Oh, my word!" cried Clarisa. "Our kitchen will burst its seams with all these good things to eat!"

"We want to make this a wonderful Christmas for all of you," Kasey told her.

Clarisa enfolded her in her arms. "Kasey, you youngsters are an absolute miracle, that's what you are."

"Oh, it's not us. We just want you to see the love of Jesus. We want to help you celebrate His birthday."

"That we'll do, child." Under her breath, Clarisa added, "Now if only we had a miracle for the rest of the year too."

"What do you mean, Clarisa?" asked Kasey.

"Oh, nothing, dear. I shouldn't have said anything. I don't want to spoil your day."

"But how could you spoil it? What do you know, Clarisa, that we should know?"

Clarisa drew her off to one side and said confidentially, "I should keep mum about this, I suppose, but I can't bear to see these poor people lose the only security they've got."

"But how? How could they lose it?"

"The city's been out here to look things over. They say if some changes aren't made, this building might be condemned."

"Condemned? Why? It looks fine to me."

"Well, yes, maybe so, but the roof is bad. It leaks something awful, and there's dry rot in the wood, and termites too, I guess. And, of course, the plumbing needs lots of work. Don't forget, Kasey, this place is older than most of our residents."

"But doesn't the city help support Shady Oaks, or charitable organizations, or something?"

"Not nearly enough, dear. Not enough to make the kind of repairs we need to stay in business." She shook her head sadly. "I hate to say it, but I think our days here may be numbered."

"But can't you let people know? Maybe they would help. Maybe someone could write an article for the newspaper about Shady Oaks and ask people to contribute."

Clarisa smiled tolerantly. "You're a dear to think of it, Kasey, but no one's going to take much interest these days in an old broken-down house filled with forgotten people."

"But there has to be something we can do," said Kasey urgently. "We just have to think of something! Maybe we can—"

Before she could finish, Ryan approached and touched her arm. "Listen, Kasey, everyone's having a great time, but I don't see Olive Solomon." He looked at Clarisa. "Is she sick? Or just being stubborn again?"

"No, not sick. You guessed it—stubborn. She's in her room. Refuses to celebrate Christmas. Said she'd come out when the party is over."

"But she's got to join us," said Kasey. "I have a special present for her."

Clarisa nodded thoughtfully. "Why don't you take it in to her, Kasey? Maybe you can persuade her to come out."

"I'll sure try."

Minutes later, Kasey walked down the long, narrow hallway and knocked timidly on Olive Solomon's door. There was a faint, toneless, "Yes, what is it?"

Kasey replied, "It's me, Mrs. Solomon. I have something for you."

The wispy voice said, "I'm resting, child. Come back later."

"Please, Mrs. Solomon. I'll just be a minute."

"All right. Come in, if you must. It's not locked."

Tentatively, Kasey entered the cramped, dimly lit room with its yellowed wallpaper and faded lace curtains. Wrapped in a shawl, Olive Solomon sat in a straight-back rocker with a worn photo album on her lap. "I'm not in the mood for partying," she snapped, "if that's what you've come for."

"I came to give you this," said Kasey, handing her a small, brightly wrapped package.

"A Christmas present?" scoffed Olive. "I don't believe in Christmas, young lady."

"But I do. Please open it. I picked it out just for you."

The ancient, austere woman grudgingly took the gift and picked at the wrappings with tremulous fingers. Moments later she held up a delicate polished cedar music box. She lifted the lid and listened to the fragile melody, her eyes glazing with unshed tears.

"It's playing 'Music Box Dancer,'" said Kasey softly. "I thought that tune might cheer you up."

"It's very nice," said Olive, dabbing at her eyes with her hanky. "But you shouldn't have bought it. I have nothing to give you in return."

"But I don't want anything. I—I just want to be your friend."

Olive looked up skeptically. "Why would a young girl like you want to be friends with an old woman like me?"

"Because I miss my grandparents," Kasey blurted. "They live far away, and I never see them anymore. And—and because you love music like I do."

Olive's lined face clouded with a deep, unsettling darkness. "I hate music," she said caustically.

"But I don't understand. They say—Clarisa says you were once an opera singer. She says you were famous. You must have loved music once."

Olive stared down at her gnarled, arthritic hands. "Yes, once. Once I loved my music. It was my life."

"What happened?" Kasey asked gently.

"That is none of your business, child."

"I—I'm sorry." Kasey took an uncertain step backward and wondered if she should leave now. Obviously this solitary woman wanted nothing to do with an awkward, tongue-tied teenager. But something indefinably mysterious about the proud, venerable lady drew Kasey, kept her from turning and fleeing. Kasey touched the corner of the old album on Olive Solomon's lap and asked, "Were you looking at pictures of your family?"

Olive's hands clutched the tattered book. "I have no family," she said abruptly.

"But you have photos—"

"Yes, photos," said Olive. "That is all I have left."

"Would you—may I see them?"

Slowly Olive opened the album and pointed to a faded picture of a bearded man in a dark suit. "That is my husband, Sol," she said. "Everyone called him Sol, but his given name was Jacob. Jacob Solomon. He was a fine man, a very wise man."

"And very handsome," said Kasey. "You must have been very happy together."

"Yes," she said faintly. "But that was long ago. My Sol has been dead nearly twenty years now."

"And you have no other family?" asked Kasey, pulling a straight-back chair over beside Olive and sitting down.

The crevices in Olive's forehead and around her mouth deepened with pain. "No one. No one before me or after me. All are gone."

Kasey couldn't keep the question back. "What happened to them?"

Olive Solomon eyed Kasey solemnly for a long moment, a strange, cryptic expression moving over her face, as if she might cry, or shout in anger, or utter important words with the wisdom of the ages in them.

Kasey sat at attention, sensing that whatever this lonely woman said would remain with her for the rest of her life.

"I do not talk about myself," said Olive matter-of-factly. "I tell no one what I have seen, the terrible things I have known. I keep these things to myself. But I will tell you, only you, because you take the time to look at me. You take the time to listen."

Carefully she pushed back her shawl and rolled up the sleeve of her sweater. She rubbed her fingers over a mark on her inner forearm. "Do you know what this is, child?"

Kasey looked closer. "It looks like a tattoo—several numbers."

"Yes," said Olive, her voice hardening. "It is the number I was forced to wear as a Jew under the rule of Hitler."

Kasey caught her breath in astonishment. "You—you were a prisoner in the—the concentration camps?"

"Yes, child. I, and my mother and father, and my brothers and sisters."

"But you—you escaped—how?"

Olive Solomon fixed her gaze on the far wall, as if glimpsing afresh the private, unspeakable horrors of her past. "How did I escape, you ask?" Her voice ebbed to an anguished whisper. "My music."

"What?" said Kasey. "Your music? I don't understand."

Tears rolled down Olive's wrinkled, leathery face. Her voice was tremulous. "In those days, the Nazis spared some Jews who possessed special talents. Scientists, musicians, artists, singers. I sang for them, child. Do you understand? I sang to stay alive. I sang for the murderers of my parents and my brothers and my sisters."

Kasey stared in stunned silence at the grieving, indomitable Olive Solomon—the crepe-paper face lost in a halo of fuzzy, silver gray hair, the stooped, sagging body, and the legs thick as stumps. Kasey knew, with startling certainty, that someday when she herself was a little old lady, she would still remember this moment, the imposing presence and shrewd, steely toughness of Olive Solomon.

Kasey remained motionless, silent. She could think of nothing to say, nothing to balance the enormity of what Olive Solomon had just confided. She felt as if she had trespassed on private property and stumbled upon something unutterable, beyond her comprehension. Then, on impulse, fighting back her own mounting tears, Kasey slipped out of her chair, threw her arms around Olive Solomon, and hugged her tight.

# 16

When Kasey returned to the Christmas celebration in the Shady Oaks living room, she found Ryan leading a round of carols while, one by one, the residents shuffled or wheeled over and hung their handmade ornaments on the fragrant, towering blue spruce.

Clarisa slipped over beside Kasey and asked, "How's Mrs. Solomon?"

"We had a good talk," said Kasey, "but she still won't come out."

"Well, you did what you could," said Clarisa. "Now join the party, and have a good time."

Kasey sat down next to Miss Brummett, a spritely octogenarian who sat tapping her toes to the music.

When Ryan spotted Kasey, he paused and said, "Hey, folks, here's our favorite pianist. Now we can really make this place hum!"

Later that evening, as Ryan drove Kasey home, she told him about her visit with Mrs. Solomon. "I sure wish I knew how to help her, Ryan. She's so sad, but she doesn't want to hear anything about God. She blames Him for the terrible things that happened to her, and she blames herself even more. It's weird, Ryan, but she feels guilty because she wasn't killed with the rest of her family. And she hates her music because that's what saved her."

"She told you all that?"

"Not exactly, but I figured it out from what she did say."

"What are you—some kind of amateur shrink?" he teased.

"No, Ryan. But it's strange. I just feel like I really understand Mrs. Solomon, like there's this connection between us, like maybe I'm the first person in years she's opened up to."

Ryan reached for Kasey's hand. "She's a smart lady, picking you for a friend. I guess that makes me smart too."

"Well, if you're smart, then I'm lucky," said Kasey. "I love having you for my friend."

He lifted her hand to his lips. "Friend, yes, and maybe just a little bit more?"

They drove in comfortable silence for a few moments. Then Kasey said, "I talked to Clarisa Huckabey tonight too, Ryan."

"Yeah? So?"

"Well, she told me some disturbing things. She said the city came out and inspected the house, and, Ryan, this is terrible, but they might actually condemn Shady Oaks."

He looked sideways at her. "No way! They can't take Shady Oaks from those old folks."

"Honest, that's what Clarisa said. The house is so old, and the roof leaks, and the plumbing's bad. But, Ryan, if they close Shady Oaks, where will all the people go?"

"Search me. Man, that's lousy. Somebody better do something."

"But who? Clarisa says there's just not enough money to keep things going. And there's no one willing to help."

"I'd help, but I only work part-time at minimum wage."

"I've been trying to think of something all evening, some way to make the community aware of the special people at Shady Oaks. Then maybe people would want to help them."

Ryan nodded. "Yeah, I tell you, those folks were in rare form tonight. Did you hear the way they sang? Some of those people are pretty talented."

"Like Mrs. Pinkelman," said Kasey. "She was in vaudeville. And did you know, some of the others were entertainers too? Mrs. Tisdale used to play the violin, and Mr. Griley played the accordion. Mrs. Hyson was a drama coach and gave readings from Shakespeare."

"Hey, it's too bad they can't do a little song and dance to let people know they're here."

Kasey pumped Ryan's arm excitedly. "Why can't they? It would be perfect. It's the obvious answer, Ryan!"

He glanced momentarily from the road. "What are you talking about? What's the answer?"

"A talent show! Don't you see? We can get the Shady Oaks residents to put on a gala talent show for the whole community. We can even sell tickets and invite the press. It'll be a regular media event."

"Get real, Kasey. Think of all the work and time it would take. And all the help we would need!"

"But, Ryan, we could get help. We could get our church youth groups and the kids at school—"

"But where would we hold a program like that? Shady Oaks certainly isn't big enough."

"OK. Try this. There's the Community Center downtown. People rent it for all sorts of things. My dad could check it out for us."

Ryan still sounded dubious. "I don't know, Kasey. Do you really think the people at Shady Oaks would want to get up on stage and—well, you know—maybe make fools of themselves?"

"Ryan, that's just it. We know those people—what different backgrounds they've had, what interesting lives they've lived. Age doesn't change that. I bet they'd welcome a chance to show the world they're the same people they always were."

"I suppose it would give some of them a chance to shine again, try out the old vocal cords, ham it up a little—"

"And we wouldn't pressure anyone," said Kasey, "but if they wanted to participate, we'd find something for them to do."

"Sure," said Ryan, catching her enthusiasm, "those who couldn't perform could sew costumes or paint sets or simply encourage the others."

"Then you do think it would work?"

"It's a crazy, wonderful idea, Kasey, but the real test will be what our friends at Shady Oaks think of it."

The next weekend, when Kasey and Ryan visited Shady Oaks, they tried out their idea on Clarisa, then on the residents. The response was lukewarm at first, but gradually interest sparked and faded eyes glinted with the light of resurrected dreams and fired imaginations.

"Looks like I'd better dust off my violin," said Mrs. Tisdale.

"And my trusty old accordion," said Mr. Griley.

"Perhaps I could recite a passage from Shakespeare," said Mrs. Hyson, her voice swelling with dramatic resonance as she proclaimed, "To be or not to be, that is the question. Whether 'tis nobler—"

Mrs. Pinkelman spoke up. "If my friend Mr. Dowling will join me, I'll do the Abbott and Costello routine 'Who's on First?'"

Mr. Dowling smiled slyly. "I'd be honored, Mrs. Pinkelman."

Miss Brummett looked over at Olive Solomon and said, "What about Olive? She was famous once. She should sing."

Olive stood stiffly, positioned her cane, and made her way toward the hallway. "I won't stand for such folly," she muttered. "You'll all make buffoons of yourselves. I won't be part of it."

As a murmuring rebuff rose from the residents, Ryan silenced them with, "Remember, no one should feel obligated to participate in the program just as no one should feel left out. Feel free to join in or just sit back and enjoy!"

So it was settled. The talent show was on.

Kasey realized with a jolt that she had her work cut out for her.

And as she might have guessed, the months of January and February turned out to be the busiest of her life. She divided her time between piano practice and rehearsals of the "Good Time Shady Oaks Players," as the residents jovially tagged themselves. Kasey was struck by the fact that her life had never seemed so full, so purposeful. Almost forgotten were the anxieties and regrets of leaving her comfortable hometown behind for the fast-paced life in Springfield.

Both Kasey and Ryan were delighted by the enthusiasm and, surprisingly, the professionalism of their venerable friends at Shady Oaks. With spunk and determination the oldsters dusted off their talents and polished their routines. Their dedication rivaled that of performers half their age.

Kasey invited her friend Jenny Clegg to organize a signing choir for those who couldn't sing. Several who were terrified at the prospect of singing before a crowd were thrilled with the chance to perform the songs with their hands. Kasey even persuaded Selena Hubbard to be her "assistant director," in charge of running errands, scheduling rehearsals, and handling publicity. Selena was—as Kasey learned—a loner in search of a cause. She thrived on her responsible position and praised Kasey for giving their friendship a second chance.

Kasey was, in fact, rather proud of the way things were working out. She was finally attaining a measure of success in every area of her life. Not only were the residents at Shady Oaks depending on her to draw out their long dormant talents, but there was also Kasey's dream of becoming a concert pianist. Every day the dream seemed more plausible, more within Kasey's grasp. Her grueling hours of practice were paying off. She had never played so well, with such precision and confidence. In fact, she sensed that at last her playing rivaled Laury Lassen's impressive performance at the all-school competition in December. Surely now Kasey stood a good chance of winning the Springfield Mozart Competition!

And, of course, there was Ryan, the boy of her dreams. Every day Kasey felt their friendship growing stronger, sweetened by fond glances, occasional kisses, and lengthy, companionable conversations. Best of all, he was always there for her, cheering her on.

As the long winter months yielded to the first fragile signs of spring, Kasey put the finishing touches on the piece she would play for the piano competition. The big day was March 15, just two days before the Shady Oaks Talent Show. Two of the most important events of her life were scheduled for the same week, but Kasey didn't mind. She was ready to show the world what she could do.

And what the old-timers could do! She and Ryan had managed to rally a motley but unforgettable group of singers, actors, musicians, and comedians from Shady Oaks. These brave senior citizens would offer their unsuspecting city a charming hodgepodge of vaudeville antics, romantic ballads, country-Western hits, and rousing show tunes, mixed with a sprinkle of Shakespeare and Keats, Laurel and Hardy. And Kasey would perform too, playing several of her favorite pieces, including Beethoven's "Ode to Joy."

"It's all coming together," she told Ryan excitedly, two days before the piano contest. They were on their way home from the final rehearsal at the civic auditorium, where the competition would be held. "I really feel confident about my playing, Ryan. I have a feeling I'm going to win, don't you? And the talent show—isn't it incredible how well the people are doing? This is going to be a wonderful week for all of us."

Ryan nodded. "Say, Kasey, have you heard any of the other contestants play?"

"No. They've got us running through our numbers in separate rooms. I guess they want the contest to be a surprise to all of us."

He took his eyes off the road long enough to grin at her. "I'll be on the front row rooting for you, Kasey. You know that."

"Do you really think I'll win, Ryan? No, wait, don't answer that. You might be prejudiced. But whatever happens, I know I'm better than Laury Lassen was last December."

"Really? I'm impressed. But you must admit Laury was good."

"Yeah, sure. She won. But I bet she hasn't touched a piano since. You know how she's always bragging about not practicing, as if it's something to be proud of."

Ryan reached over for Kasey's hand. "Listen, kiddo, did you ever think you might be misjudging Laury?"

"Not for a minute. Why?"

"Because—well, did it ever occur to you that maybe she's lying about not practicing?"

"Why would she do that?"

Ryan shrugged. "I don't know. Maybe so if she fails she'll save face. Maybe her indifference is a cover-up for how much winning really matters to her. Maybe she's trying to hide her real feelings."

"Which are?"

"Fear—anxiety."

"Oh, Ryan, give me a break! Laury Lassen—afraid? If she really cared about the piano, she'd practice, take the whole thing seriously."

Ryan was silent a moment. Then he said quietly, "Listen, Kasey, maybe it's time you knew something about Laury Lassen."

She eyed him quizzically. "What?"

"You'll see." He turned right at the next signal and drove several blocks. "In case you're wondering, Kasey, this is Laury's neighborhood."

"Yeah, I figured as much. The houses all look as snooty as Laury. So what are we doing here?"

Ryan pulled up in front of a large, ranch-style house and turned off the engine. "Roll down your window, Kasey, and listen."

She did, but all she heard was the wind whistling through the trees. "What am I supposed to hear? I don't see what—"

"Listen, Kasey. Hear it?"

She listened. "No—uh, wait, yeah, I hear—I hear music, someone playing the piano!" She looked at Ryan. "Laury?"

"Right. She must have just left the rehearsal like we did, and yet she's already back home practicing. Hear it? And anytime you drive by her house, you're likely to hear the same thing."

"What are you saying, Ryan?"

"I'm saying she gave you a big fat line about not practicing. The truth is she's totally dedicated to her music. She gets up before dawn to practice and stays up past midnight playing. She's obsessed with it, Kasey. She lives and breathes her music."

Kasey shook her head, her heart pounding, her palms suddenly moist. "No, Ryan, that's impossible. It can't be. Laury bragged about not practicing, about piano being no big deal."

"That's just it, Kasey. Piano is the biggest deal in Laury's life. But she doesn't want anyone else to know."

"That's crazy, Ryan. If she's so dedicated, why wouldn't she want us to know how hard she works?"

"Like I said, she's scared to death of failing. But if she knew I told you the truth, she'd have my head."

Kasey sucked in a sharp breath. "I can't imagine Laury being afraid. She's the coolest person I know—so cool she's practically icy. Nothing scares her, Ryan."

"Sure, that's the facade she wears. That's what she wants everyone to think. But I know the real Laury. Don't forget, we grew up together."

"You—you almost sound like you admire her," said Kasey softly.

"I—I guess I do. I mean, she acts Loony Tunes sometimes, but underneath she's a tough, gritty girl. She has to be."

"What do you mean?"

112

"I mean, her parents. They ride her hard. They expect her to be their golden girl, Miss Perfect. They've never loved her just for herself. I could see that even when I was a little kid. And Laury knew it too. If she wanted her folks' affection, she really had to shine. That's why winning is everything to her."

Kasey gazed in fascination at the beautiful house that echoed with faint strains of a piano concerto. "I—I never thought of Laury like that. I just saw her as sort of an enemy."

Ryan nodded. "I know she hasn't been very nice to you, but I think she's jealous of your talent. She's afraid you'll outshine her."

"You—you really think so? That totally blows my mind."

Ryan turned the ignition key. "What I've told you about Laury is strictly between us, OK? I just wanted you to know that you're not competing against some scatterbrained flake. If—when!—you win over Laury, I want you to know you've really accomplished something."

# 17

This place is humungous!" said Kasey as she stepped from the backstage wings and peeked through the velvet curtains at the mammoth auditorium. The cavernous room was teeming with people filing down the aisles and taking their seats. Kasey looked over at a fellow contestant—a tall blonde from Woodcrest, a rival school—and said, "How come the auditorium looks bigger with an audience than it did empty?"

"I don't know," said the girl, "but my knees are knocking like a jackhammer."

"Mine too," said Kasey. "Everyone in Springfield must be here tonight."

"Goodness, Kasey, don't tell me you're nervous," said a light, lilting voice behind her.

Kasey turned abruptly and forced a smile at Laury Lassen. The slender brunette looked cool and composed, her makeup flawless, her sultry eyes glinting with merriment. "Hi, Laury," said Kasey. "You, uh, sure look happy. Looks like you're ready to conquer the world."

"Conquer the world? Not tonight," Laury purred. "But I am ready to win the scholarship."

"Well, good luck," Kasey mumbled, feeling suddenly awkward and self-conscious. Why was it?—when she was around Laury she felt as if she had her clothes on backwards or spinach between her teeth.

"Good luck?" Laury echoed contemptuously. "I really don't need luck, Kasey. After all, I have talent on my side. But I do wish *you* luck. I'm sure you can use it."

"I don't believe in luck," said Kasey dryly. "I believe in hard work. But I guess we've both learned that, haven't we?"

A flicker of curiosity crossed Laury's face. "Well, I must admit I've practiced a little more than usual for this competition."

"Me too. So may the better one win."

"How generous of you, Kasey," said Laury thickly. "Ryan told me how sweet and sincere you are. I guess he's right."

"Ryan?"

"Oh, yes. He talks about you quite often. He's such a darling, isn't he? When he feels sorry for people, he takes them under his wing like wounded little birds, until they can fly again. Why, he's done that for those poor old people at Shady Oaks. And he's done that for you, hasn't he?—and look how you've blossomed." Her sugarcoated voice took on a slightly menacing tone as she pursed her plum-red lips. "But now Ryan thinks you're ready to fly on your own again, so let him go, Kasey. Don't be a clinging vine."

Kasey stared dumbfounded at Laury. "Are you saying—did Ryan tell you that—that I'm a clinging vine?"

"Oh, no, he's much too nice to say it. But that's how he feels. Surely you can sense when someone's just being nice to you. But whatever you think, get this, Kasey. Ryan is *my* friend. He was mine long before he met you."

"He—he doesn't belong to anyone, Laury," Kasey stammered. She could feel her face flushing and her pulse racing with sudden heat and anger. Her voice quavered. "Why can't Ryan be friends with both of us?"

Laury rolled her eyes impatiently. "Because I don't like sharing, Kasey, whether it's Ryan—or the spotlight. Think about that while you're out on stage showing what a poor little country girl can do." With that, Laury pivoted sharply, fluffed back her mane of burnished brown hair, and strutted off with her chin high.

Watching Laury sashay away, Kasey felt weak in the knees, as if she'd just endured physical combat. She couldn't have felt more bruised and battered if Laury had slapped her. Was there any truth to what Laury had said about Ryan? Surely not. Surely Laury's cutting words were only her jealousy speaking. But then again . . .

The tall blonde contestant was suddenly shaking Kasey's arm, telling her, "Come on, get in your place. The program's beginning!"

Kasey followed wordlessly and took her seat backstage with the other pianists. She could hear the muted voice of the announcer on stage as he introduced the first contestant. Kasey listened. She sat primly in her chair in the new dress her mother had bought for this occasion, her hands folded in her lap. She imagined herself playing the piece, freed her mind to ride the music, sail with it, riding the crests, dipping into the valleys. The pianist was superb, flawless. When the performance was done, the applause crescendoed, and Kasey, listening, felt drained. Could she play her piece with such mastery and eloquence?

She closed her eyes, sighed deeply, and attempted to psych herself up for her own performance. She felt the tension rise along her spine and through her shoulder blades. No, relax, she told herself. Stay loose, keep calm.

Another contestant. This time Kasey tried to shut out the music; it stole too much of her own energy. But she couldn't miss the fact that this performance, too, was exceptional. Who were these impressive performers? Obviously no one from Springfield High, for Kasey and Laury had already proved they were the best there.

*But I'm not the best here*, Kasey realized with a terrifying jolt. *I'm not better than the pianists I've heard so far. Am I even as good? Oh, God, don't let me get out on stage and make a fool of myself!*

Kasey sat motionless through three more performances. Still four to go before her turn to play. She stared down at her sheet music and saw that the sweat from her palms was wrinkling it. *Oh, great! At this rate I won't even be able to turn the pages. They'll just sit there and droop. Or what if I just sit there and droop?*

As the minutes passed, Kasey's heart began to hammer. The pounding sounded in her ears above the lilting music. Her legs were feeling numb, her fingers tingly. She felt as if she might remain like this forever, sitting, waiting, caught in a timeless freezeframe of petrified panic. Another contestant played, and then Laury Lassen stood up with solemn regality and walked out on stage. Kasey heard the announcer say, "Ladies and gentlemen, we present Miss Laury Lassen, playing *Danse Macabre*, by Camille Saint-Saens, a symphonic poem based on a poem by Henri Cazalis."

Kasey knew she couldn't ignore Laury's performance, so she listened intently, allowing her imagination to soar with Laury's dancing fingers. Kasey was familiar with the piece and its chilling death theme. As the haunting cadences rose and fell, Kasey pictured shrouded skeletons dancing in dark shadows, their bones rattling in measured beats. Then, with a flourish, Laury played the final trill, and the audience applauded vigorously.

*She's done it again*, thought Kasey.

And then suddenly it was Kasey's turn. Someone was nudging her shoulder and saying, "Go. Get out there. You're on!"

Kasey stood up and moved toward the stage. Somehow she felt strangely disconnected from her body, as if she might not actually be moving at all but still sitting in her chair imagining that it was her turn to go on. Was this real? Was any of this real?

She slipped through the heavy velvet draperies that separated the audience from the private, chaotic backstage world of machinery and props. She paused just out of sight until she heard the announcer intone, "Ladies and gentlemen, Miss Kassandra Carlone, playing *Clair de Lune*, by Claude Debussy."

Squinting against the glaring overhead lights, Kasey strode toward the gleaming grand piano on center stage. Her heels clacked noisily on the polished hardwood floor. It was the only sound she heard in the enormous auditorium.

As she sat down at the piano, Kasey glanced nervously out at the audience. The faces blurred and merged like splashes of paint on a canvas. She couldn't pull her gaze away, couldn't break the hypnotic spell that bound her. What was wrong? Why did she feel so immobilized— as if the entire world had come to a grinding halt and was waiting now for her to make the next move.

For the first time in her life Kasey truly wished she were invisible. What awful insanity had prompted her to place herself in this bright, excruciating circle of attention? Her mouth turned to cotton, and her heart boomed in her ears. She felt dizzy, disoriented. Would she faint? Would she faint gracefully or land in a disheveled heap, a shell-shocked pianist fallen in the line of duty to be unceremoniously dragged away by some beefy stagehand?

She sat motionless, her eyes locked on the endless sea of faces. She thought she might die of mortification. Or her heart might explode inside her. A paralysis of shame gripped her body, mind, fingers, and hands. How could she even hope to play the scales, let alone a difficult classical composition? It was no longer a question of would she play her piece perfectly, but would she play it at all?

Kasey realized she was losing track of time. Had she sat here for hours, minutes, or mere seconds? She considered jumping up and dashing off the stage, but she would just make more of a spectacle of herself. No, she had to get through this; somehow she had to make her fingers work, had to begin playing.

Then, from the hushed, waiting maze of humanity, a boy's voice (a friend of Laury's perhaps?) shattered the stillness. "Hey, country girl, if you can't cut it on stage, go back to the farm!"

A murmur rippled over the audience. Several people began to clap. Kasey grew more frantic. *Who was the audience siding with?* she wondered. *That rude boy or her?* She blinked back hot angry tears and forced herself to begin playing. Her fingers moved over the keys, but they felt stiff, unresponsive. She was forcing the music, not flowing with it. The emotion was flat. *Oh, God, I'm not doing my best*, she thought wildly. *How am I going to get through this?*

Then the nightmare deepened. She missed a note. She would lose points for that. How could she continue when her world was quietly collapsing around her? How could she pretend that nothing was wrong?

Then, another mistake. A wrong note! More points against her. She would come in last for sure. If she came in at all!

As Kasey's trembling fingers moved over the keyboard, she sensed the audience's mounting anxiety. *They're not with me*, she thought desperately. *They're waiting for me to flub again.*

Finally, after what seemed forever, it was over. Kasey stood and bowed slightly while the audience applauded. Her legs felt like overcooked spaghetti. She tried to smile, but her cheerful expression toppled. Her composure was about to shatter. Kasey Carlone had failed in the worst possible way, publicly, for all the world to see. Even as she bowed again, perfunctorily, she was drowning in her own humiliation. She knew her life would never be the same again.

# 18

Kasey listened numbly as the judge announced the winner and four runners-up of the Springfield Mozart Competition. Fourth and fifth places went to a boy and girl from Woodcrest High. Third place went to a senior girl from Springfield High. Then the judge intoned, "The first runner-up is—Miss Laury Lassen of Springfield High."

Kasey looked quickly over at Laury. She looked stricken (could the great Laury Lassen accept anything less than first place?), but she managed to walk over to the podium and accept her trophy for second place.

Irrationally, feverishly, Kasey prayed, hoping against hope, that she might still win first place, the $5000 scholarship, the chance to play at the state finals. She held her breath, the tension a painful knot in her chest, as the announcer declared, "And the grand winner of the Springfield Mozart Competition is—Harold Jackson from Woodcrest High!"

Kasey's hopes plummeted like ducks shotgunned in flight, like helium balloons pelted by buckshot, like kites ripped by a rainstorm. Reason returned, and dark reality descended. It was over, her failure complete. She, who had dreamed of and nearly tasted "winner's gold," had not even placed.

After the program, as the audience dispersed, Kasey pushed through the crowd in search of her mom and dad. Finding them, she fell into her father's arms and buried her face against his chest while he whispered over and over, "Don't cry, Kasey. We're proud of you, baby."

"You were very brave, Kasey," her mother assured her. "You overcame your fear and played anyway. That's what counts."

Even Keith was unusually kind. "You have a lot of guts, Sis. I couldn't have faced this crowd the way you did."

Kasey dried her eyes and shook her head. "I just feel like such a fool, such a total failure. I never want to play in front of an audience again."

"I know it hurts, honey, but you'll change your mind," said her mother. "Give it a little time. You'll be better than ever."

"No, I won't. I won't ever forget tonight or how awful I feel." Kasey glanced around. "Where's Ryan? Didn't he sit with you?"

"Yeah, he did," said Keith. "But right after the program he took off. I—well, I saw him leave with—Laury Lassen."

Kasey stared wide-eyed at Keith. "He left with—Laury?"

"Yeah." Keith lowered his voice. "I hate to say it, but they looked kind of cozy. As they walked out, he had his arm around her."

Kasey clasped her father's arm. "Take me home, Dad. Please!"

All the way home Kasey kept telling herself that this must be a dream, a terrible nightmare, and any moment she would awaken and it would still be the morning of the competition, and she would play perfectly, the way she knew she could, and Ryan would be there beside her when they announced that she had won. The events had happened that way in her mind for weeks now; she knew them so well they were more real than this new, terrible reality that her mind still couldn't quite contain. Was it possible? She had lost the piano competition, had humiliated herself in front of the entire city, and now Ryan was gone; Ryan had returned to Laury just as Laury had said he would.

What was left? What was there to hold on to now? If only she could escape back to Middleton, back to her dear, kind grandparents and her safe, predictable life there. If only she could erase all these painful, wonderful, roller-coaster months in Springfield! Silently, accusingly, she prayed, *Oh, God, why did You do this to me? If You love me, why are You hurting me this way?*

As soon as Kasey arrived home, she went straight to her room, threw herself on her bed, and sobbed until she couldn't cry anymore. Aloud, she uttered brokenly, "I'll never play the piano again. I'll never like another boy. I'll never leave this room until I die!"

But shortly, there was a knock on her door. "Go away," she said at first, then relented and said, "Come in."

Her parents entered. Her mom sat beside her on the bed; her dad settled in the rocking chair. "Can we talk, honey?" said her dad.

She stared sullenly at the floor. "There's nothing to talk about. I messed up my whole life tonight, and it's too late to change anything now."

"That's not so, Kasey."

"But it is, Dad. I was out of my league and too stupid to know it. I freaked out. I was so scared, I just froze."

"That can happen to anyone, Kasey," said Mom.

"I'm not anyone. I'm me. It happened to me!" Kasey pushed her hair back from her face. It was limp and wet with her tears. "I'm a total failure, Mom. How can I ever face anybody again?"

"You're not a failure, Kasey," said Dad. "A failure is someone who never tries in the first place, someone who never takes risks and therefore never grows."

Kasey absently twisted a strand of hair around her finger. "I was so sure I was going to win. I prayed and had faith, and I was going to give God the glory. What went wrong? Why is God punishing me when I was just trying to do my best?"

Her dad sat forward and propped his elbows on his knees. "He's not punishing you, Kasey. I don't have all the answers for you, but I do know that God loves you and has special things planned for you."

Tears filled her eyes again. "All I ever wanted to do was become a concert pianist—and I worked so hard and came so close!"

"Listen, Kasey," said Mom, "nothing has changed. Your dreams can still come true. This was just one evening out of all your life. It doesn't have to mean anything more than what you decide it means."

"It means I'm a loser, Mom. I'll never be good enough—"

"Good enough for what, Kasey? You were good enough to compete with the best in the city—and brave enough to walk out on that stage and play in spite of your fears. Next time, Kasey, you'll know what to expect. You won't be so afraid—"

"There won't be a next time," said Kasey defiantly.

Her mother placed a gentle hand on her shoulder. "I'm not trying to minimize your feelings, Kasey. I know you're disappointed. It's only natural. But it doesn't mean you're a loser or a failure. Maybe you were just trying to do too much. You've worked so hard with the people at Shady Oaks and spent so many hours practicing the piano. You were exhausted. I could see it. So could your dad."

"Stop making excuses for me, Mom. I know what I know. I failed. Don't try to whitewash it." Kasey stood up and walked over to the window, her back to her parents. Finally, she choked out, "The worst part is—I lost Ryan too. And now the kids at school will never accept me either. I'll just be a big joke to everyone."

Kasey's father joined her at the window. Softly he said, "Listen, honey, you're not the only one in this house who's had to deal with feelings of failure lately."

Kasey slowly met his gaze. "I—I'm not? Who—?"

Dad's eyes were warm with compassion. "Your mom. Me."

"You and Mom? You're kidding, Dad. You're not failures."

"I agree. But that doesn't mean we haven't experienced failure occasionally. I've had some rough adjustments to make in my new job, and I've failed a few times, but I'm learning from my mistakes, and I know I'm eventually going to succeed."

"Same here, Kasey," said Mom. "When we first moved here, I was unnerved by some of our 'liberated' neighbors. They seemed to look down on full-time homemakers like me. I even wondered if I was a failure, until I remembered I was doing what God wanted me to do. I realized that's what counts. Now I get along fine with our busy, modern neighbors, and I think they even envy me a little."

"Your mom's right," said Dad. "If you measure yourself by the world's definition of success, you'll never be happy. They say be rich, popular, glamorous, and powerful, and you'll be a success. But that's not so. By that definition, Jesus Himself wasn't a success."

"Dad, please, I don't want one of your sermons tonight."

"I know, Kasey. But it might help to think about what Jesus went through. He was God Himself and could have come to earth as a king, but He was born in a stable among animals and died on a cross between thieves. He didn't run with the popular crowd. He attracted the ragtag of humanity and stirred such hatred among the ruling class that they put Him to death. Talk about failure!—or at least what the world considered failure."

"I already know the story, Dad," said Kasey solemnly.

"Sure, you know it. It's the greatest story in history. But stop and think what it meant for Jesus to pay the price for our salvation—to taste every kind of failure by man's definition. The point is, He succeeded by God's standards."

Kasey looked up at her father. "What do you mean?"

"I mean, Jesus loved God, trusted Him, obeyed Him, and honored Him. That's real success, Kasey. With priorities like that, a person could turn the world upside-down. Jesus did. So did the early disciples. You can too."

"Me? No way. What can I do?"

"You've already begun," said her mother. "Look what you've accomplished with the needy people at Shady Oaks, the confidence in themselves you've given them. Let them see Jesus in you, and you'll never be a failure—not by God's definition, anyway."

"Oh, no!—the folks at Shady Oaks!" exclaimed Kasey. "I almost forgot them! They're expecting me to direct them at the dress rehearsal tomorrow night."

"Of course," said Mom. "The talent show is just two days away."

"I've got to go see them," said Kasey, dashing over to the bureau and grabbing the alarm clock. "What time is it?"

"Kasey, what's the matter?"

"Oh, no! It's too late!" she lamented. "It's after ten. But I've got to go tell them—"

"Tell them what? What's wrong, Kasey?"

"The talent show! They've got to get someone else. I can't direct it, can't play for it."

"Kasey, really, you can't just quit like that—"

"Can't I?" Kasey countered sharply. "Listen, Mom, I'm not going near a stage or playing the piano for anyone—ever again!"

# 19

The next morning, Kasey rode with Keith to school as usual, but when he pulled into the senior parking lot, she said, "You go on in. I've got an errand to run."

He gave her a suspicious glance. "You're not going to school?"

"Yeah. Later. But right now I have to drive over to Shady Oaks. There's something I've gotta do."

"Yeah, I get the picture. You're gonna dump on all those old people who are counting on you."

"I'm not either. I—I'm going to save them the embarrassment of having me represent them at the talent show."

"Yeah, that's what I said. You're gonna dump on them, leave 'em hanging after all the work they've done."

"Am not!" Kasey glared at Keith as he turned off the engine and tossed her the keys. "I just don't want to spoil their show the way I spoiled the piano competition. Is that such a crime?"

Keith opened his door and stepped out of the car. "Cut the pity party, Kasey. Admit it. One little goof and you've turned yellow-bellied."

"One *major* goof, Slimeface," she snapped. "Take a hike, OK?"

Kasey arrived at Shady Oaks just as the residents were finishing breakfast. Quietly, she drew Clarisa Huckabey off to one side and said, "I've got to talk to you about the talent show." She spilled out the details of last night's piano fiasco in halting phrases, then concluded, "So I think you should get someone else to lead the show. I'd just make a mess of it, and I—I can't play in public again."

"But who? How? It's too late, Kasey," said Clarisa helplessly.

"What's this about the show?" asked Mrs. Smolin, appearing suddenly from around the corner with Mr. Griley and Mrs. Pinkelman. "We didn't mean to eavesdrop, but we caught a few words . . ."

Clarisa told them briefly what Kasey had told her. One by one their eyes clouded, and their expressions fell.

"We can't have a show without you, Kasey," said Mrs. Pinkelman.

Mr. Griley rasped, "I've got my accordion all ready to go."

"I know, and I'm sorry. I'm so sorry," said Kasey, fighting back tears. "Maybe Ryan can help you. He'll still be here."

"But you're the one who's bolstered our confidence, Kasey."

"I know, and I think you'll all do a wonderful job, but—"

The news spread quickly among the residents.

Even as Kasey groped for words, Olive Solomon hobbled over and looked her directly in the eye. Gripping her cane with a stern patriarchal air, Olive stood her ground in

129

her frumpish button-down sweater, long skirt, beige support hose, and heavy flat black shoes. "Are you telling us the talent show is canceled?" she demanded.

"No, uh, not exactly," Kasey stammered.

"Then what? Tell me."

"Ryan and Jenny and Selena will be here—"

"And so will you, young lady," declared Olive indignantly.

"But I—I—"

"Listen to me, child." Olive's voice was resonant with gritty conviction. "People have run out on me all my life. I'm used to it, expect it, in fact. But not you, young lady. I have watched you for months now, and that is not your way. Oh, I know. I've scoffed at your music and your simple faith, but I am no fool. I've seen what you've done. You've made us believe in ourselves again. We are depending on you!"

Kasey's voice broke in a sob. "But you don't understand, Mrs. Solomon. Last night I failed—!"

But Olive had more to say. "You youngsters—you come in here every week singing hymns and spouting Scripture about your God, like you've found something in your little handful of years that we have missed in four score or more. Now maybe you have. Maybe we can learn a thing or two from you, just like you can learn from us. But before you come here and tell us what we need in our lives, you better be good and sure it works for you. So you go and think hard about this, Miss Kassandra Carlone. Either your God cares about you, or He doesn't. Which is it?"

"He—yes, I mean, I don't know—I can't—!" Confused, tongue-tied, and fighting back tears, Kasey turned and ran from the room and out the door of Shady Oaks to her car. She drove aimlessly around the city until lunchtime, wondering how her entire life could have fallen apart so swiftly. How could she have been so on top of things one day and be so devastated the next? Did God really care about her? If so, where was He now when she needed Him?

At noon, Kasey drove to Springfield High, parked in the senior lot, and made her way to the cafeteria. She had to find Jenny Clegg. Jenny always had a special way of looking at things, as if she could see right to the heart of what really mattered.

Jenny was at her usual table, finishing a globby pudding thing optimistically called dessert. When Kasey gently touched her shoulder, Jenny whirled around and stared up in surprise. "Kasey! Where were you?" Her fingers were already moving swiftly to express what her tongue managed with difficulty. "I looked for you all morning!"

"I—I went out to Shady Oaks."

"But why?"

Kasey glanced around uneasily. Was everyone watching, remembering her blundering performance, laughing behind her back? "Are you through here? Can we go somewhere and talk?"

"Of course." She held up her dessert. "Do you want some Surprise Delight? It's better than usual."

"No, thanks. I'll resist the temptation today."

Jenny disposed of her tray, then followed Kasey outside. As they walked toward a nearby park, Kasey said, "I guess you were at the piano competition last night."

"Yes," said Jenny. "I wanted very much to be on stage with you, feeling the vibrations as you played, telling you how it sounded to me, cheering you on."

"I wish you had. I would have done better."

Jenny nodded. "I saw the pain in your face. I prayed for you."

"It didn't help. I messed up. God really set me up for a fall."

Jenny looked questioningly at Kasey. "God did it?"

"Well, no, not exactly. But He sure could have kept me from making a total fool of myself."

"Who says you made a fool of yourself? Ryan told me you played very well."

"I didn't even place."

"Neither did most of the contestants. Only five could place."

Jenny's argument struck Kasey with its simple, irrefutable logic. So she changed the subject. "You talked with Ryan today?"

"Yes," said Jenny, signing gracefully with her hands. "He was looking for you. He has something important to tell you."

"Yes, I know," said Kasey. "Something I don't want to hear. And I—I must tell you something you won't want to hear, Jenny." Reluctantly Kasey explained that she would not direct or play for the Shady Oaks talent show. "Please understand. I can't bear to go on stage again so soon. All my confidence is gone. It just hurts too much right now."

"Why does it hurt?" Jenny asked softly.

"Why? How can you ask that?" cried Kasey. "It hurts because I wanted so much to be a success—and I failed miserably!"

Jenny nodded toward a park bench. "Can we sit down?"

"Sure. We can stay here all day. The last thing I want is to face the kids at school."

Jenny's fingers flew expressively, an index finger at her temple, then circling her face, her hands crossing her heart and pointing to Kasey.

"Yes, I understand," said Kasey tonelessly. "You're telling me you care about me and want me to be happy."

Jenny pointed toward the sky and repeated the gestures.

"Yes. You're saying God loves me and wants me to be happy too. I believe it, but I don't feel it."

"Not happy," said Jenny. "Happy depends on circumstances. God wants you to have joy. Joy doesn't depend on circumstances. It just is. It comes from doing what God wants you to do no matter what happens."

Kasey shook her head slowly. "I'm sorry, Jenny. Right now that just sounds like a bunch of gobbledegook. I'm not joyful or happy. Don't you see? I'm totally thrashed. I feel like a dork or some lowlife flunky. When I lost it last night something inside me died."

Jenny nodded, her eyes full of warmth and sympathy. "I know what it means to fail, Kasey. People expect me to fail because I cannot hear. But sometimes something has to die before something better can be born."

"You're still talking in riddles," said Kasey somberly.

"Not riddles, Kasey. God's point of view." Jenny signed as she verbally articulated each word. "God sees failure and success different from you and me, and different from the kids at school."

"Yeah, I suppose so, but . . ."

Jenny went on, her face animated as she spoke. "You have a big heart of love for old people and little children —and for lonely fat people and lonely deaf people—for the people no one else takes time to know. That is a rare, rare gift, Kasey. It makes you very special. Special to God. Special to others. Special to me."

Kasey's chin began to quiver. She blinked away her tears and rolled her eyes heavenward. "Oh, Jenny," she sighed in wonderment, "you always know just the right thing to say!"

# 20

Kasey returned to school for her afternoon classes, but she dreaded facing Ryan Dimarco in English. As she might have expected, he was his usual chipper self, informing her that all the tickets for the talent show were sold and that the media promised to cover the event. "Looks like we're all set for dress rehearsal," he said. "I'll pick you up about seven, OK?"

She looked away. "No, I'm not—I mean, it's not necessary."

"Why not? How will you get there?"

"I-I'm not sure I'm going," she said in a small, thin voice.

"Not going? Of course, you're going. We can't have rehearsal without you."

She shook her head, flustered. "I don't want to talk about it now. Later, all right?"

"Yeah, sure," he answered, frowning. "In fact, I've tried to get hold of you all day. I've got something to talk to you about."

"I think I already know," she said quietly.

"Tell you what. I'll drive you home from school. We'll talk then." He hesitated. "Listen, I'm sorry I didn't get a chance to tell you what a good job you did in the piano competition."

Kasey covered her mouth with her hand. "Oh, Ryan, please, don't be kind. I can't bear it."

"I'm not, Kasey. You played very well. I know you didn't win, but then neither did Laury. You were both up against some really stiff competition. But that doesn't mean you should be ashamed of your performance. That's what I told Laury too."

Kasey didn't want to hear another word about Laury, so she opened her textbook and stared down at it. "We'd better be quiet," she told Ryan. "It's time for class to start."

After school, as Ryan drove her home, Kasey kept waiting for the ax to fall. Or maybe Ryan was going to wait until after the talent show to tell her that he had chosen Laury over her. What had Laury said before the competition? *I don't like sharing Ryan—or the spotlight!*

"Now what's this nonsense about you not going tonight?" he asked. "You're not getting cold feet, are you—after all our work?"

"You and Jenny and Selena can manage without me," she murmured. "And lots of the kids have already volunteered to be ushers and help with costume changes and all that. You don't need me."

"Our friends at Shady Oaks need you to buoy them up—you know, give them that last minute shot of adrenaline to spur them on. And we all want to hear you play the pieces you've rehearsed."

"No, thanks," she declared. "I had enough of that last night."

"Speaking of last night, Kasey, that's what I wanted to talk to you about," said Ryan as he pulled into her driveway.

*Oh, boy, here it comes!* she thought. "I already know, Ryan."

"Know? What do you mean?"

"I know you left the competition with Laury."

He turned in his seat to face her. "I'm sorry I didn't get a chance to tell you, but I really didn't have any choice."

"I'd say you made your choice when you two left together."

He gave her a puzzled glance. "You sound like you already know about Laury. Did she tell you?"

"Maybe. But I'd rather hear it directly from you."

"OK, but you've got to keep it confidential."

"How can I do that? It'll be obvious to the whole school."

Ryan frowned. "Kasey, are we talking about the same thing?"

"You and Laury—"

"Laury's suicide attempt," said Ryan. "Isn't that what she told you about?"

Kasey stared in astonishment at Ryan. "Suicide? Laury tried to commit suicide?"

"I thought you said she told you."

"No, uh, that was something else. When did Laury try to, uh—"

"Last year. She overdosed on sleeping pills. Her parents found her and rushed her to the hospital. They pumped her stomach, and she was OK—physically, anyway. Emotionally, it's another story."

"I never dreamed that Laury—I mean, she's so cool and beautiful and all-together. Why would she do such a terrible thing?"

136

"Because Laury can't accept the fact that she's only human, Kasey. She doesn't know the love and peace Jesus gives. She's only got herself. And she has to be perfect at everything. She'll never be happy, Kasey, because she'll never be able to live up to her own expectations."

"So I guess she was pretty upset last night—you know, about coming in second in the piano competition."

Ryan nodded. "There's nothing wrong with second place, but with Laury it was either all or nothing. She couldn't handle losing."

"Yeah, I know the feeling," said Kasey under her breath.

"So that's why I left with her. I was afraid of what she might do. We went back to her house and talked half the night. I think I helped her gain a little perspective about things."

Kasey sat at attention. "Wait a minute, Ryan. Back up a little. You're saying you left with Laury because you thought—you were afraid she might try to kill herself?"

"Yes. I felt responsible. Like I told you, her parents don't take to second place very well. Neither does Laury. We're old friends, practically like brother and sister. I'm the only friend she's got who knows about her past—"

"Oh, Ryan!" Kasey almost laughed aloud. "I thought—"

"What? That I wanted to be with her instead of you? No way!" He reached over and took her hand. "It's just that I knew you could handle losing better than Laury could. You've got the Lord—and your family sticks by you—"

Kasey hung her head. "Oh, Ryan, if you only knew—"

"And like my dad says," Ryan continued, "when you're in the will of God, there's no such thing as failure. Right, Kasey?" He opened the car door. "Anyway, about tonight—"

"Can you pick me up?"

"But you said some crazy thing about not going."

She opened her door and stepped out. "Are you kidding? I wouldn't miss tonight for the world!"

Later, in her room, as Kasey dressed for the rehearsal, she whispered confidentially, "Lord Jesus, forgive me for coming unglued about the piano contest. It still hurts an awful lot, but I think it's made me smarter about some things."

She took off her glasses, breathed on the lenses, and cleaned them with a tissue. "Lord, I'm trying hard to figure things out. I guess I wanted to be popular and admired by people who know nothing about what You want for my life. But I'm beginning to understand. You've given me successes I've never even counted—my friends at Shady Oaks, the little kids I play for at church and in the neighborhood, and Ryan, Jenny, and Selena . . ."

She put on her glasses and stared at her reflection. "I'm still scared to death to go back on stage, but I know it's what You want me to do. So, please, help me, Jesus. Give me the courage to do what's right. And, please, bless our rehearsal tonight."

# 21

The next night—a crisp, clear, star-studded evening—the Shady Oaks Talent Show opened to a full house.

"Hey, look, the Community Center is packed out!" said Selena as she joined Kasey backstage. "Isn't it fantastic?"

"Talk about success in a major way! There's standing room only," said Ryan as he handed Kasey the performance schedule.

"And the TV station is here filming," said Kasey breathlessly. "They figure this will make a great human interest piece."

"And the coverage should help bring in plenty of donations to save Shady Oaks," said Ryan. He looked around and declared, "Is everyone ready to put on a show?"

"Jenny's rehearsing the signing choir one last time," said Selena. "They're all wearing pastels. They look so springlike."

The bountiful Mrs. Pinkelman, in a red dress that matched her cheeks, a lace shawl, and a wide-brimmed flowered hat, bustled over to Kasey and burbled, "Is my hat on straight? Do the flowers show? Am I wearing too much rouge?"

"You look wonderful," said Kasey, brushing her cheeks lightly with a Kleenex and adjusting the hat slightly.

Mrs. Pinkelman clasped her hands together in a gesture of pure ecstasy. "Oh, this is just like the night I sang with George Burns. Ah, that man—what a dreamboat! He was so dashing and debonair!"

White-haired Mr. Suttles shuffled over beside Mrs. Pinkelman and said gallantly, "Will I do this evening, dear lady? I can croon a tune and crack a joke or two as well as the next fellow."

"You'll have your chance to prove it, Mr. Suttles," said Ryan. "You're on right after Mrs. Pinkelman."

"Don't forget," said the billowy Mrs. Pinkelman, "that Mr. Dowling and I are doing our Abbott and Costello routine too."

"What about me?" asked Mrs. Tisdale. "My violin's ready."

"And I'm all set with my accordion," said Mr. Griley.

Mrs. Hyson drifted by in a long black evening gown. "To be or not to be," she trilled, her arms wafting on the air like fluttery bird wings.

Ryan chuckled. "I think we're ready to put on a show. What do you think, Kasey?"

"We'd better be. It's time to start. I hope the guys doing the lights know what to do."

"They're all set. Selena's getting everyone in place. The place is sold out. I'm ready. You're ready. Let's do it!"

Kasey breathed a prayer: "Please, Jesus, let me do OK!"

A motley group of octogenarians that tagged themselves the Venerable Skewbald Band opened the program with "Stardust" and "Alexander's Ragtime Band." Mrs. Pinkelman followed with a twittery rendition of "Listen to the Mockingbird." Then Mr. Suttles, in his railroad cap and overalls, did a soft-shoe to "Sweet Georgia Brown."

Finally, it was Kasey's turn to play. As she walked toward the piano, she thought desperately, *Oh, Lord, this is a replay of the other night. What if I tighten up? What if I can't perform? What if I spoil everything? Jesus, please help me to honor You!*

She sat down at the piano and put her music in place, then poised her fingers over the keys. Her heart hammered nervously. Once again it was just Kasey Carlone confronting an endless sea of faces. Would she survive this moment? *When you fall off a horse you get right back on again and ride . . .*

She began to play Beethoven's triumphant "Ode to Joy." As her fingers skipped and pranced over the keys, she recalled what Jenny had said about happiness and joy being two different things. *Happiness depends on circumstances. Joy comes from being obedient to the will of God.* Yes, this evening was God's will for Kasey. Even in this moment she knew her playing was pleasing to Him.

Suddenly she realized she had finished the piece and the audience was applauding vigorously. "More, more!" someone shouted from the back. "Bra-vo!"

Kasey stood and bowed, then sat back down and began to play *Clair de Lune*, the piece she had played for the piano competition. But this time she plunged herself into the emotion of the music and savored the very act of performing. She was one with the music and one with the Lord, offering Him a symphony of praise, and the joy was nearly overwhelming.

Afterward, the audience gave her a standing ovation. Kasey stood trancelike, incredulous, overjoyed.

Then, unexpectedly, Ryan strode onto the stage and took the microphone. "Ladies and gentlemen," he said in his clear, tenor voice, "we have a special surprise for this young lady who inspired and directed tonight's program. A good friend of Kasey Carlone's is going to sing a song just for her, a song to let her know how much she means to all of us."

Kasey looked up in bewilderment. "There's no singer next on the program, Ryan."

"I know," he whispered. "Come sit down and watch this one." With a mysterious smile, he led her down into the audience to a front-row seat. As she sat down, she spotted an incredible sight—a stubby, bent woman with a wreath of gray hair and the steadfastness of the ages etched in her wrinkled, timeworn face. "Ryan, look," Kasey cried. "What is Olive Solomon doing up there on center stage?"

"Wait and see."

"She's taking the microphone, Ryan. You mean, you got her to sing?"

"No," he whispered. "*You* got her to sing."

Olive spoke in a solid, rich, slightly accented voice. "Ladies and gentlemen, I will sing for you *La Boheme-mi Chiamano Mimi*, by Giacomo Puccini. First, I tell you, I have not sung for an audience for over thirty years. But tonight I sing for my little friend Kasey. She has invested much time and effort to remind me that, with love and appreciation, the human spirit can still flourish in an aged, failing body."

Olive Solomon drew in a deep breath and began to sing in perfect Italian. Her full, dramatic soprano voice ranged from long phrases of crystal-clear lightness to melting, sumptuous tones that stirred the senses. When she finished, the audience went wild.

Olive stood proudly, unmoving, until the applause died down. Then she said in a clear, forceful voice, "Now, for you kind people I will sing 'The Lord's Prayer.' Long ago I stopped singing because I had no song, but Kasey gave me back my song. Even better, she gives me a new song. She makes me know Someone still cares. God loves me through her."

As Olive's strong, lilting voice rang with the majestic strains of "Our Father, who art in heaven," Kasey understood, in one of those rare, crystallized moments, that as long as she walked faithfully with her Lord and obeyed Him, no matter what else happened, she would never have to fear failure again.

Moments later, as Olive Solomon trilled the final amen of the Lord's Prayer, she reached out her scarred arm to Kasey. Impulsively, Kasey bounded out of her chair, dashed up onto the stage, and wrapped her arms around Olive.

Behind her, Kasey could hear Ryan shouting above the applause, "That'a girl, Kasey! That's the way to go!"